THE TRAIN
WAS ON TIME

THE TRAIN
WAS ON TIME

Heinrich Böll

TRANSLATED FROM THE GERMAN
BY LEILA VENNEWITZ

Northwestern University Press
EVANSTON, ILLINOIS

Northwestern University Press
Evanston, Illinois 60208-4170

Originally published in German under the title of *Der Zug war pünktlich* in a volume entitled *1947 bis 1951*, copyright © 1949, 1950, 1951 by Friedrich Middelhauve Verlag, Cologne. English translation copyright © 1970 by Leila Vennewitz. Northwestern University Press edition published 1994 by arrangement with Kiepenheuer & Witsch, Cologne-Berlin and Leila Vennewitz. All rights reserved.

Printed in the United States of America

10 9 8 7 6 5 4 3

ISBN 0-8101-1123-3

Library of Congress Cataloging in Publication Data

Böll, Heinrich, 1917–
   [Zug war pünktlich. English]
   The train was on time / Heinrich Böll ; translated from the German by Leila Vennewitz.
      p. cm. — (European classics)
   ISBN 0-8101-1156-X (alk. paper). — ISBN 0-8101-1123-3 (pbk. : alk. paper)
   1. World War, 1939–1945—Fiction. I. Title. II. Series:
European classics (Evanston, Ill.)
PT2603.0394Z4513   1994
833'.914—dc20   93-49332
                                                      CIP

Translator's Acknowledgment
I am deeply indebted to my husband,
William Vennewitz, for his never-failing advice
and assistance in this translation.
LEILA VENNEWITZ

I have known many adventures in my time: the creation of postal routes, Sahara rebellions, South America . . . but war is not really an adventure at all, it is only a substitute for adventure. . . . War is a disease. Like typhus.

Antoine de Saint-Exupéry,
Pilote de Guerre

As they walked through the dark underpass they could hear the train rumbling up to the platform overhead, and the resounding voice came smoothly over the loudspeaker: "The troop-train now arriving from Paris will depart for Przemysl via...."

Then they had climbed the steps to the platform and were standing by the leave-train from which beaming soldiers were emerging, weighed down with huge packages. The platform quickly emptied, it was the usual scene. At some of the windows stood girls or women or a very silent, grim-faced father ... and the resounding voice was telling people to hurry. The train was on time.

"Why don't you get on?" the chaplain asked the soldier anxiously.

"Get on?" asked the soldier, amazed. "Why, I might want to hurl myself under the wheels, I might want to desert ... eh? What's the hurry? I might go crazy, I've a perfect right to, I've a perfect right to go crazy. I don't want to die, that's what's so horrible—that I don't want to die." His voice was cold and hard, as if the words were pouring from his lips like ice. "Don't say any more! I'll get on all right, there's always a spot somewhere ... yes ... yes, don't mind me, pray for me!" He grasped his pack, boarded the train through the nearest door, let down the window from inside, and leaned out, while overhead the resounding voice hung like a cloud of mucus: "The train is now leaving...."

"I don't want to die!" he shouted. "I don't want to die, but the terrible thing is that I'm going to die ... soon!" The black figure on that cold gray platform retreated farther and farther into the distance . . . farther and farther, until the station was swallowed up by night.

Now and again what appears to be a casually spoken word will suddenly acquire a cabalistic significance. It becomes charged and strangely swift, races ahead of the speaker, is destined to throw open a chamber in the uncertain confines of the future and to return to him with the deadly accuracy of a boomerang. Out of the smalltalk of unreflecting speech, usually from among those halting, colorless goodbyes exchanged beside trains on their way to death, it falls back on the speaker like a leaden wave, and he becomes aware of the force, both frightening and intoxicating, of the workings of fate. To lovers and soldiers, to men marked for death and to those filled with the cosmic force of life, this power is sometimes given, without warning; a sudden revelation is conferred on them, a bounty and a burden . . . and the word sinks, sinks down inside them.

As Andreas was slowly groping his way back into the center of the car, the word *soon* entered him like a bullet, painlessly and almost imperceptibly penetrating flesh, tissue, cells, nerves, until at some point it caught, like a barbed hook, exploded, and ripped open a savage wound, making blood pour out . . . life, pain. . . .

Soon, he thought, and felt himself turning pale. At the same time he did all the usual things, almost unconsciously. He struck a match, lighting up the heaps of sitting, stretched out, sleeping soldiers who lay around, across, under, and on top of their luggage. The smell of stale tobacco smoke was mixed with the smell of stale sweat and that strangely gritty dirt which clings to all soldiers in the mass. The flame of the dying matchstick flared up with a final hiss, and in that last glow he saw, over by the narrowing corridor, a small empty space. He carefully picked his way toward it, his bundle tucked under one arm, his cap in his hand.

Soon, he thought, and the shock of fear lay deep, deep. Fear and absolute certainty. Never again, he thought, never again will I see this station, never again the face of my friend, the man I abused right up to the last moment . . . never again. Soon! He reached the empty space, set his pack carefully on the floor in order not to wake the sleeping men around him, and sat down on it so he could lean back against a compartment door. Then he tried to arrange his legs as comfortably as possible; he stretched the left one carefully past the face of one sleeping soldier, and placed the right one across a piece of luggage that was shielding the back of another. In the compartment behind him a match flared up, and someone began to smoke silently in the dark. By turning slightly to one side he could see the glowing tip of the cigarette, and sometimes, when the unknown man drew on it, the reflection spread over an unfamiliar soldier's face, gray and tired, with bitter creases in it, starkly and terribly sober.

Soon, he thought. The rattle of the train, it was all so familiar. The smell, the desire to smoke, the feeling he had to smoke. The last thing he wanted to do was sleep. The somber outlines of the city moved past the window. Somewhere in the distance searchlights were raking the sky, like long spectral fingers parting the blue cloak of the night . . . from far away came the firing of antiaircraft guns . . . and those darkened, mute, somber houses. When would this Soon be? The blood flowed out of his heart, flowed back into his heart, circling, circling, life was circling, and all this pulse beat said was: Soon! He could no longer say, no longer even think: "I don't want to die." As often as he tried to form the sentence he thought: I'm going to die . . . soon.

Behind him a second gray face now showed up in the glow of a cigarette, and he could hear a subdued, weary murmuring. The two unknown men were talking.

"Dresden," said one voice.

"Dortmund," the other.

The murmuring continued, became more animated. Then another voice swore, and the murmuring subsided again; it petered out, and again there was only one cigarette behind him. It was the second cigarette, and finally this one went out too, and again there was this gray darkness behind and beside him, and facing him the black night with the countless houses, all mute, all black. Only in the distance those silent, uncannily long, spectral fingers of the searchlights, still groping across the sky. It seemed as if the faces belonging to those fingers must be grinning, eerily grinning, cynically grinning like the faces of usurers and swindlers. "We'll get you," said the thin-lipped, gaping mouths belonging to those fingers. "We'll get you, we'll grope all night long." Maybe they were looking for a bedbug, a tiny bug in the cloak of the night, those fingers, and they would find the bug. . . .

Soon. Soon. Soon. Soon. When is Soon? What a terrible word: Soon. Soon can mean in one second, Soon can mean in one year. Soon is a terrible word. This Soon compresses the future, shrinks it, offers no certainty, no certainty whatever, it stands for absolute uncertainty. Soon is nothing and Soon is a lot. Soon is everything. Soon is death. . . .

Soon I shall be dead. I shall die, soon. You have said so yourself, and someone inside you and someone outside you has told you that this Soon will be fufilled. One thing is sure, this Soon will be in wartime. That's a certainty, that's a fact.

How much longer will the war go on?

It can last for another year before everything finally collapses in the East, and if the Americans in the West don't attack, or the British, then it will go on for another two years before the Russians reach the Atlantic. They will attack, though. But all in all it will last another year at the very least, the war won't be over before the end of 1944. The way this whole apparatus is built up, it's too obedient, too cowardly, too docile. So I may still have anything from one second to one year. How many seconds are there in a year? Soon I'm going to die, before the war is over. I shan't ever know peacetime again. No more peacetime. There'll be no more of anything, no music . . . no flowers . . . no poetry . . . no more human joy; soon I'm going to die.

This Soon is like a thunderclap. This little word is like the spark that sets off the thunderstorm, and suddenly, for the thousandth part of a second, the whole world is bright beneath this word.

The smell of bodies is the same as ever. The smell of dirt and dust and boot polish. Funny, wherever there are soldiers there's dirt. The spectral fingers had found the bug. . . .

He lit a fresh cigarette. I'll try and picture the future, he thought. Maybe it's an illusion, this Soon, maybe I'm overtired, maybe it's tension or nerves. He tried to imagine what he would do when the war was over. He would . . . he would . . . but there was a wall he couldn't get over, a totally black wall. He couldn't imagine anything. Of course he could force himself to complete the sentence in his mind: I'll go to university . . . I'll take a room somewhere . . . with books . . . cigarettes . . . go to university . . . music . . . poetry . . . flowers. But even as he forced himself to complete the sentence in his mind he knew it wouldn't happen. None of it would happen. Those aren't dreams, those are pale, colorless thoughts devoid of weight, blood, all human substance. The future has no face now, it is cut off somewhere; and the more he thought about it the more he realized how close he was to this Soon. Soon I'm going to die, that's a certainty that lies between one year and one second. There are no more dreams. . . .

Soon. Maybe two months. He tried to imagine it in terms of time, to discover whether the wall rose this side of the next two months, that wall he would not be going beyond. Two months, that meant the end of November. But he can't grasp it in terms of time. Two months: an image that has no power. He might just as well say: three months or four months or six, the image evokes no echo. January, he thought. But the wall isn't there at all. A strange, unquiet hope awakens: May, he thought with a sudden leap ahead. Nothing. The wall is silent. There's no wall anywhere. There's nothing. This Soon . . . this Soon is only a frightening bogey. November, he thought. Nothing! A fierce, terrible joy springs to life. January: January of next year, a year and a half away—a year and a half of life! Nothing! No wall!

He sighed with relief and went on thinking, his thoughts now racing across time as over light, very low hurdles. January, May, December! Nothing! And suddenly he was aware that he was groping in a void. The place where the wall rose up couldn't be grasped in terms of time. Time was irrelevant. Time had ceased to exist. And yet hope still remained. He had leaped so splendidly over the months. Years. . . .

Soon I'm going to die, and he felt like a swimmer who knows he is near the shore and finds himself suddenly flung back into the tide by the surf. Soon! That's where the wall is, the wall beyond which he will cease to exist, will cease to be on this earth.

Krakow, he thought suddenly, and his heart missed a beat as if an artery had twisted itself into a knot, blocking off the blood. He is on the right track—Krakow! Nothing! Farther. Przemysl! Nothing! Lvov! Nothing! Then he starts racing: Cernauti, Jassy, Kishinev, Nikopol! But at the last name he already senses that this is only make-believe, make-believe like the thought: I'll go to university. Never again, never again will he see Nikopol! Back to Jassy. No, he won't see Jassy again either. He won't see Cernauti again. Lvov! Lvov he'll see again, Lvov he'll reach alive! I'm mad, he thought, I'm out of my mind, this means I'll die between Lvov and Cernauti! What a crazy idea . . . he forced himself to switch off his thoughts and started smoking again and staring into the face of the night. I'm hysterical, I'm crazy, I've been smoking too much, talking, talking for nights on end, days on end, with no sleep, no food, just smoking, it's enough to make anyone lose their mind. . . .

I must have something to eat, he thought, something to drink. Food and drink keep body and soul together. This damn smoking all the time! He started fumbling with his pack, but while he peered toward his feet in the dark, trying to find the buckle, and then began rummaging around in his pack where sandwiches and underwear, tobacco, cigarettes, and a bottle of schnapps all lay in a heap, he became aware of a leaden, implacable fatigue that clogged his veins . . . he fell asleep . . . his hands on the open pack, one leg—the left—next to a face he had never seen, one leg—the right—across someone's luggage, and with his tired and by now dirty hands resting on his pack he fell asleep, his head on his chest. . . .

He was awakened by someone treading on his fingers. A stab of pain, he opened his eyes; someone had passed by in a hurry, bumped him in the back and trodden on his hands. He saw it was daylight and heard another resounding voice hospitably announcing a station name, and he realized it was Dortmund. The man who had spent the night behind him smoking and murmuring was getting out, cursing as he barged along the corridor; for that unknown gray face, this was home. Dortmund. The man next to him, the one whose luggage his right leg had been resting on, was awake and sat up on the cold floor of the corridor, rubbing his eyes. The man on the left, whose face his left foot was resting against, was still asleep. Dortmund. Girls carrying steaming pots of coffee were hurrying up and down the platform. The same as ever. Women were standing around weeping; girls being kissed, fathers . . . it was all so familiar: he must be crazy.

But, to tell the truth, all he knew was that the instant he opened his eyes he knew that Soon was still there. Deep within him the little barb had drawn blood, it had caught and would never let go now. This Soon had grabbed him like a hook, and he was going to squirm on it, squirm until he was between Lvov and Cernauti. . . .

Like lightning, in the millionth part of a second it took him to wake up, came the hope that this Soon would have disappeared, like the night, a bogey in the wake of endless talking and endless smoking. But it was still there, implacably there. . . .

He sat up, his eye fell on his pack, still half open, and he stuffed back a shirt that had slipped out. The man on his right had let down a window and was holding out a mug into which a thin, tired girl was pouring coffee. The smell of the coffee was horrible, thin steam that made him feel queasy; it was the smell of barracks, of army cookhouses, a smell that had spread all over Europe . . . and that was meant to spread all over the world. And yet (so deep are the roots of habit) and yet he also held out his mug for the girl to fill; the gray coffee that was as gray as a uniform. He could smell the stale exhalation from the girl; she must have slept in her clothes, gone from train to train during the night, lugging coffee, lugging coffee. . . .

She smelled penetratingly of that vile coffee. Perhaps she slept right up close to the coffeepot as it stood on a stove to keep hot, slept until the next train arrived. Her skin was gray and rough like dirty milk, and wisps of her scanty, pale-black hair crept out from under a little cap, but her eyes were soft and sad, and when she bent over to fill his mug he saw the charming nape of her neck. What a pretty girl, he thought: everyone will think she's ugly, and she's pretty, she's beautiful . . . she has delicate little fingers too . . . I could spend hours watching her pour my coffee; if only the mug had a hole, if only she would pour and pour, I would see her soft eyes and that charming nape, and if only that resounding voice would shut up. Everything bad comes from those resounding voices; those resounding voices started the war, and those resounding voices regulate the worst war of all, the war at railway stations.

To hell with all resounding voices!

The man in the red cap was waiting obediently for the resounding voice that had to say its piece, then the train got under way, lighter by a few heroes, richer by a few heroes. It was daylight but still early: seven o'clock. Never again, never ever again will I pass through Dortmund. How strange, a city like Dortmund; I've passed through it often and have never been in the town itself. Never ever will I know what Dortmund is like, and never ever again will I see this girl with the coffeepot. Never again; soon I'm going to die, between Lvov and Cernauti. My life is now nothing but a specific number of miles, a section of railway line. But that's odd, there's no front between Lvov and Cernauti, and not many partisans either, or has there been some glorious great cave-in along the front overnight? Is the war suddenly, quite suddenly, over? Will peace come before this Soon? Some kind of disaster? Maybe the divine beast is dead, assassinated at last, or the Russians have launched an attack on all fronts and swept everything before them as far as between Lvov and Cernauti, and capitulation. . . .

There was no escape, the sleeping men had woken up, they were beginning to eat, drink, chat....

He leaned against the open window and let the chill morning wind beat against his face. I'll get drunk, he thought, I'll knock back a whole bottle, then I won't know a thing, then I'll be safe at least as far as Breslau. He bent down, hurriedly opened his pack, but an invisible hand restrained him from grasping the bottle. He took out a sandwich and quietly and slowly began to chew. How terrible, to have to eat just before one's death. Soon I'm going to die, yet I still have to eat. Slices of bread and sausage, air-raid sandwiches packed for him by his friend the chaplain, a whole package of sandwiches with plenty of sausage in them, and the terrible thing was that they tasted so good.

He leaned against the open window, quietly eating and chewing, from time to time reaching down into his open pack for another sandwich. Between mouthfuls he sipped the lukewarm coffee.

It was terrible to look into the drab houses where the slaves were getting ready to march off to their factories. House after house, house after house, and everywhere lived people who suffered, who laughed, people who ate and drank and begat new human beings, people who tomorrow might be dead; the place was teeming with human life. Old women and children, men, and soldiers too. Soldiers were standing at windows, one here, one there, and each man knew when he would be on the train again, traveling back to hell....

"Hey there, mate," said a husky voice behind him, "want to join us in a little game?" He swung round: "Yes!" he said without thinking, at the same time catching sight of a deck of cards in a soldier's hand: the soldier, who was grinning at him, needed a shave. I said Yes, he thought, so he nodded and followed the soldier. The corridor was deserted except for two men who had taken themselves off with their luggage to the vestibule, where one of them, a tall fellow with blond hair and slack features, was sitting on the floor, grinning.

"Find anybody?"

"Yes," said the unshaven soldier in his husky voice.

Soon I'm going to die, thought Andreas, squatting down on his pack, which he had brought along. Each time he put down the pack his steel helmet rattled, and now the sight of the steel helmet reminded him that he had forgotten his rifle. My rifle, he thought, it's standing propped up in Paul's closet behind his raincoat. He smiled. "That's right, mate," said the blond fellow. "Forget your troubles and join the game."

The two men had made themselves very snug. They were sitting by a door, but the door was barricaded, the handle tightly secured with wire, and luggage had been stacked up in front of it. The unshaven soldier took a pair of pliers out of his pocket—he was wearing regular blue work pants—he took out the pliers, fished out a roll of wire from somewhere under the luggage, and began to wind fresh wire still more tightly around the door handle.

"That's right, mate," said the blond fellow. "They can kiss our arses till we get to Przemysl. You're going that far, aren't you? I see you are," he said when Andreas nodded.

Andreas soon realized they were drunk; the unshaven soldier had a whole battery of bottles in his carton, and he passed the bottles around. First they played blackjack. The train rattled, daylight grew stronger, and they stopped at stations with resounding voices and stations without resounding voices. It filled up and emptied, filled up and emptied, and all the time the three men stayed in their corner playing cards.

Sometimes, at a station, someone outside would rattle furiously at the locked door and swear, but they would only laugh and go on with their game and throw the empty bottles out of the window. Andreas didn't think about the game at all, these games of chance were so wonderfully simple there was no need to think, your mind could be somewhere else. . . .

Paul would be up by now, if he had slept at all. Maybe there had been another air-raid alarm, and he hadn't had any sleep. If he had slept, then it could only have been for a few hours. He must have got home at four. Now it was almost ten. So he had slept till eight, then got up, washed, read mass, prayed for me. He prayed for me to be happy because I had denied human happiness.

"Pass!" he said. Marvelous—you just said "Pass!" and had time to think. . . .

Then he would have gone home and smoked cigarette butts in his pipe, had a bite to eat, some air-raid sandwiches, and gone off again. Some place or other. Maybe to a girl having an illegitimate baby by a soldier, maybe to a mother, or maybe to the black market to buy a few cigarettes.

"Flush," he said.

He had won again. The money in his pocket made quite a packet now.

"You're a lucky bastard," said the soldier who needed a shave. "Drink up, my friends!" He passed the bottle around again, he was sweating, and beneath the mask of coarse joviality his face was very sad and preoccupied. He shuffled the cards . . . a good thing I don't have to shuffle them. I need one more minute to think about Paul, to concentrate on Paul, tired and pale; now he's walking through the ruins and praying, all the time. I gave him hell, you should never give anyone hell, not even a sergeant. . . .

"Three of a kind," he said, "and a pair." He had won again.

The other men laughed, they didn't care about the money, all they wanted was to kill time. What a laborious, frightful business it was, this killing time, over and over again that little seconds-hand racing invisibly beyond the horizon, over and over again you threw a heavy dark sack over it, in the certain knowledge that the little hand went racing on, relentlessly on and on. . . .

"Nordhausen!" proclaimed a resounding voice. "Nordhausen!" The voice announced the name of the station just as he was shuffling the cards. "Troop-train now departing for Przemysl via . . ." and then it said: "All aboard and close the doors!" How normal it all was. He slowly dealt the cards. It was already close on eleven. They were still drinking schnapps, the schnapps was good. He made a few complimentary remarks about the schnapps to the soldier who needed a shave. The train had filled up again. They had very little room now, and quite a few of the men were looking at them. It had become uncomfortable, and it was impossible to avoid overhearing the men's chatter.

"Pass," he said. The blond fellow and the unshaven soldier were sparring good-naturedly for the kitty. They knew they were both bluffing, but they both laughed, the point was to see who could bluff best.

"Practically speaking," said a North German voice behind him, "practically speaking we've already won the war!"

"Hm," came another voice.

"As if the Führer could lose a war!" said a third voice. "It's crazy to say such a thing anyway: winning a war! Anyone who talks about winning a war must already be considering the possibility of losing one. Once we start a war, that war is won."

"The Crimea's already cut off," said a fourth voice. "The Russians have closed it off at Perekop."

"That's where I'm being sent," said a faint voice, "to the Crimea. . . ."

"Only by plane, though," came the confident voice of the war-winner. "It's great by plane. . . ."

"The Tommies won't risk it."

The silence of those who said nothing was terrible. It was the silence of those who don't forget, of those who know they are done for.

The blond fellow had shuffled, and the unshaven soldier opened with fifty marks.

Andreas saw he was holding a royal flush.

"And fifty," he said, laughing.

"I'm in," said the unshaven soldier.

"Raise twenty."

"I'm in."

Needless to say, the unshaven soldier lost.

"Two hundred and forty marks," said a voice behind them, accompanied, as the sound of the voice indicated, by a shake of the head. It had been quiet for a minute while they had been battling for the kitty. Then the chatter started up again.

"Have a drink," said the unshaven soldier.

"This door business is crazy, I tell you!"

"What door?"

"They've barricaded the door, those bastards, those scabs!"

"Shut up!"

A station without a resounding voice. God bless stations without resounding voices. The buzzing chatter of the other men went on, they had forgotten about the door and the two hundred and forty marks, and Andreas gradually began to realize he was a bit drunk.

"Shouldn't we have a break?" he said. "I'd like a bite to eat."

"No!" shouted the unshaven soldier, "not on your life, we'll carry on till we get to Przemysl! No"—his voice was filled with a terrible fear. The blond fellow yawned and began muttering. "No," shouted the unshaven soldier. . . .

They went on playing.

"The 42 MG is all we need to win the war. The others have nothing like it. . . ."

"The Führer knows what he's doing!"

But the silence of those who said nothing, nothing at all, was terrible. It was the silence of those who knew they were all done for.

At times the train got so full they could hardly hold their cards. All three were drunk by now, but very clear in the head. Then the train would empty again, there were loud voices, resounding and unresounding. Railway stations. The day wore on to afternoon. From time to time they would pause for a snack, then go on playing, go on drinking. The schnapps was excellent.

"Well, it's French, after all," said the soldier who needed a shave. He seemed to need one more than ever now. His face was pallid under the black stubble. His eyes were red, he hardly ever won, but he appeared to have a vast supply of money. Now the blond fellow was winning often. They were playing chemin-de-fer, the train being empty again, then they played rummy, and suddenly the cards fell from the unshaven soldier's hand, he slumped forward and began to snore horribly. The blond fellow straightened him, gently arranging him so that he could sleep propped up. They put something over his feet, and Andreas returned his winnings to the man's pocket.

How gently and tenderly the blond fellow treats his friend! I'd never have expected it of that slob.

I wonder what Paul's doing now?

They got to their feet and stretched, shook crumbs and dirt from their laps, and cigarette ash, and flung the last empty bottle out of the window.

They were traveling through an empty countryside, left and right glorious gardens, gentle hills, smiling clouds—an autumn afternoon. . . . Soon, soon I'm going to die. Between Lvov and Cernauti. During the card game he had tried to pray, but he kept having to think about it; he had tried again to form sentences in the future and realized they had no force. He had tried again to grasp it in terms of time—it was make-believe, idle make-believe! But he had only to think of the word Przemysl to know he was on the right track. Lvov! His heart missed a beat. Cernauti! Nothing . . . it must be somewhere in between . . . he couldn't visualize it, he had no mental picture of the map. "D'you have a map?" he asked the blond fellow, who was looking out of the window.

"No," he said amiably, "but he does!" He pointed to the soldier who needed a shave. "He has a map. How restless he is. He's got something on his mind. That's a fellow with something terrible on his mind, I tell you. . . ."

Andreas said nothing and looked over the man's shoulder through the window. "Radebeul!" said a resounding Saxon voice. A decent voice, a good voice, a German voice, a voice that might just as well be saying: The next ten thousand into the slaughterhouse, please. . . .

It was wonderful outside, still almost like summer, September weather. Soon I'm going to die, I'll never see that tree again, that russet tree over there by the green house. I'll never see that girl wheeling her bike again, the girl in the yellow dress with the black hair. These things the train's racing past, I'll never see any of them again. . . .

The blond fellow was asleep now too, he had sat down on the floor beside his pal, and in sleep they had sunk against one another; the snores of one were harsh and loud, of the other soft and whistling. The corridor was deserted except for now and again someone going to the john, and occasionally someone would say: "There's room inside, you know, mate." But it was much nicer in the corridor, in the corridor you were more alone, and now that both the others were asleep he was quite alone, and it had been a terrific idea to secure the door with wire.

Everything the train's leaving behind I'm leaving behind too, once and for all, he thought. I'll never see any more of this again, never again this segment of sky full of soft gray-blue clouds, never again this little fly, a very young one, perched on the window frame and flying off now, off to somewhere in Radebeul; that little fly will stay in Radebeul, I guess . . . stay behind under this segment of sky, that little fly will never keep me company between Lvov and Cernauti. The fly is on its way to Radebeul, maybe it's flying into some kitchen heavy with the odor of potatoes boiled in their jackets and the acrid smell of cheap vinegar, where they're making potato salad for some soldier who's now free to suffer for three weeks through the alleged joys of home leave . . . that's all I'll ever see, he thought, for at that moment the train swung in a great loop and was coming into Dresden.

At Dresden the platform was very full, and at Dresden many men got out. The window faced a whole cluster of soldiers headed by a stout, red-faced young lieutenant. The soldiers were all dressed up in brand-new uniforms, the lieutenant was also in his brand-new hand-me-downs for the doomed; even the decorations on his chest were as new as freshly cast lead soldiers, they looked like complete fakes. The lieutenant grasped the door handle and rattled it.

"Open up there!" he shouted at Andreas.

"The door's closed, it won't open," Andreas shouted back.

"Don't shout at me, open up, open up at once!"

Andreas shut his mouth and glowered at the lieutenant. I'm soon going to die, he thought, and he's shouting at me. His gaze went beyond the lieutenant; the soldiers standing with the lieutenant grinned behind his back. At least the faces of these men were not new, they had old, gray, knowing faces, only their uniforms were new, and even their decorations seemed old and worn. Only the lieutenant was new from top to toe, he even had a brand-new face. His cheeks became redder still, and his blue eyes went a bit red too. Now he lowered his voice, and it was so soft, with such a soft threat in it, that Andreas had to laugh. "Are you going to open the door?" he asked. Rage was exploding from his shiny buttons. "Look at me at least!" he roared at Andreas. But Andreas did not look at him. I'm going to die soon, he thought; all these people standing around on the platform, I'll never see any of them again, not one. And he wouldn't smell that smell again either, that smell of dust and railway smoke, here at his window saturated with the smell of the lieutenant's brand-new uniform that smelled of synthetic wool.

"I'll have you arrested," roared the lieutenant. "I'll report you to the military police!"

Luckily the blond fellow had woken up. He came to the window, sleepy-eyed, stood impeccably at attention, and said to the lieutenant:

"Regret to report, sir, that the door was sealed off on the station side on account of its being defective: to prevent accidents." He delivered this in the regulation manner, briskly and submissively, it was marvelous the way he spoke, like a clock striking twelve. The lieutenant let out one more furious sigh. "Why didn't you say so?" he yelled at Andreas.

"Regret to report further, sir, that my companion is deaf, stone deaf," the blond fellow rattled off. "Head wound." The soldiers behind the lieutenant laughed, and the lieutenant turned beet-red, swung round, and went off to look for space somewhere else. The bevy of men followed him. "Stupid bastard," muttered the blond fellow after him.

I could get out here, thought Andreas as he watched the lively bustle on the platform. I could get out here, go off someplace, any place, on and on, till they caught me and put me up against a wall, and I wouldn't die between Lvov and Cernauti, I would be shot in some little village in Saxony or die like a dog in a concentration camp. But I'm standing here by the window and I feel as if I were made of lead. I can't move, I feel paralyzed, this train is part of me and I'm part of the train, this train that has to carry me to my appointed end, and the strange part about it is that I have absolutely no desire to get out here and stroll along the banks of the Elbe under those nice trees. I long for Poland, I long for that horizon as intensely, as fiercely and ardently, as only a lover can long for his beloved. If only the train would move, if only it would get going! Why is it standing here, why is it standing so long in this godforsaken Saxony, why has the resounding voice been silent for so long? I'm bursting with impatience, I'm not scared, that's the strange thing, I'm not scared, just indescribably curious and restless. Anl yet I don't want to die. I want to live, theoretically life is beautiful, theoretically life is glorious, and I don't want to get out, it's funny to think I could get out. I need only walk along the corridor, leave my useless pack behind and clear out, anywhere, stroll under trees with their fall coloring, and I go on standing here as if I were made of lead; I want to stay on this train, I have a terrible longing for the gray drabness of Poland and for that unknown stretch between Lvov and Cernauti where I have to die.

Shortly after Dresden the unshaven soldier woke too. His face was ashen under the stubble, and his eyes sadder than ever. Without a word he opened a can and began eating the meat inside, spearing lumps of it onto his fork; with it he ate some bread. His hands were dirty, and from time to time scraps of meat would fall to the floor, the floor where he would be sleeping again tonight, with its litter of cigarette butts and that accumulation of impersonal grime which every soldier seems to attract like a magnet. The blond fellow was eating too.

Andreas stood at the window and saw nothing; it was light outside and the sunshine still mild, but he saw nothing. His thoughts were seething as the train sped by the pleasant garden suburbs around Dresden. He waited impatiently for his unshaven friend to finish his meal so that he could ask him for the map. He had no idea what it was like between Lvov and Cernauti. Nikopol he could imagine, even Lvov and Przemysl ... Odessa and Nikolayev ... and Kerch, but Cernauti was only a name; it made him think of Jews and onions, of gray streets with flat-roofed houses, wide streets, and traces of administration buildings of the old Austrian Empire, neglected gardens around crumbling Imperial façades that might now be sheltering hospitals or first-aid posts; and those boulevards of Eastern Europe with their brooding charm, their squat trees, cropped to prevent the flat-roofed houses from being crushed by treetops. No treetops. . . .

That's what Cernauti would be like, but what came first, what came between Lvov and Cernauti, was something he couldn't picture at all. It must be Galicia, Lvov being the capital of Galicia. And somewhere there was Volhynia—all dark, somber names smelling of pogroms and vast gloomy estates where brooding women dreamed of adultery since they had begun to find their blubber-necked husbands repulsive. . . .

Galicia, a dark word, a terrible word, and yet a splendid word. It sounded something like a knife cutting very quietly . . . Galicia. . . .

Lvov is all right, Lvov he can visualize. Splendid and gloomy and without lightness, those cities, with bloody pasts and untamed back streets, silent and untamed.

The soldier who needed a shave threw his can out of the window, returned the loaf, from which he had been biting off mouthfuls, to his pack, and lit a cigarette. His face was sad, sad, full of remorse somehow, as if he were ashamed of the orgy of cards and boozing; he joined Andreas at the window, leaning his elbows on it, and Andreas sensed that he wanted to talk.

"Look at that, a factory," he said, "a chair factory."

"Yes," said Andreas. He saw nothing, nor did he want to see anything, only the map. "Might I," he made a great effort, "might I have a look at the map?"

"What map?" Andreas felt a deep stab of fear and knew he turned pale. Supposing this fellow didn't have any map?

"The map of Poland," he stammered, "the map of where we're going."

"Oh, that one," said the man. He bent down at once, fumbled in his pack, and handed him the folded map.

It was horrible to have the man leaning over the map with him. Andreas could smell the canned meat on his breath, which was still not quite free of the odor of digested, partially acidulated schnapps. He could smell the sweat and grime and was too wrought up to see anything; then he saw the man's finger, a thick, red, dirty, yet very good-natured finger, and the man said: "That's where I have to go." Andreas read the name of the place: "Kolomyya." Strange, now that he looked closer he could see that Lvov was not far at all from this Kolomyya...he went back ...Stanislav, Lvov...Lvov...Stanislav, Kolomyya, Cernauti. Strange, he thought; Stanislav, Kolomyya...these names evoked no definite echo. That voice inside him, that wakeful, sensitive voice, oscillated and trembled like a compass needle which cannot settle. Kolomyya, shall I get as far as Kolomyya? Nothing definite...a strange wavering of the ever-vibrating needle... Stanislav? The same quivering. Nikopol! he thought suddenly. Nothing.

"Yes," said the man, "that's where my unit is. Repair depot. I'm lucky." But it sounded as if he really meant: I'm having a terrible time.

Funny, thought Andreas. I had imagined there would be a plain in that area, a green patch with a few black dots, but the map is whitish-yellow there. Foothills of the Carpathians, he thought suddenly, and in his mind's eye he instantly saw his school, all of it, the corridors and the bust of Cicero and the narrow playground squeezed in between tenements, and in summertime the women leaning out of the windows in their bras, and the janitor's room downstairs where you could get a mug of cocoa, and the big store-room, dry as a bone, where they used to go for a quick smoke during recess. Foothills of the Carpathians. . . .

Now the man's finger was lying farther to the southeast. "Kherson," he said, "that's where we were last, and now we're moving farther back, probably as far as Lvov or right into the Hungarian Carpathians. The front's collapsing in Nikopol—I guess you heard that on the news, eh? They're wading through the mud, a retreat through mud! Must be a madhouse, all the vehicles get stuck, and when three happen to get stuck one behind the other everything on the road behind them has had it, there's no going back and no going forward, and they blow up the lot . . . they blow up the lot, and everyone has to foot-slog it, the generals too, I hope. But I bet they get flown out. . . . They ought to go on foot, on foot like the Führer's beloved infantry. Are you with the infantry?"

"Yes," said Andreas. He had not taken in much. His gaze was resting almost tenderly on this section of the map, it was yellow-ish-white with only four black dots, one big fat one: Lvov, and one slightly smaller: Cernauti, and two very little ones: Kolomyya and Stanislav.

"Let me keep the map," he said huskily, "let me keep it," without looking at the other man. He could not bear to part with the map, and he trembled at the thought that the man might say no. Many people are like that, an object suddenly becomes valuable to them because someone else would like to have it. An object that the very next moment they might throw away becomes precious and valuable and they wouldn't dream of selling it, just because someone else would like to own it and use it.

Many people are like that, but the unshaven soldier wasn't.

"Sure," he said, surprised, "it's not worth anything. Twenty pfennigs. Besides, it's an old one. Where're you heading for anyway?"

"Nikopol," said Andreas, and again he was aware of that appalling void as he uttered the word, he felt as if he had cheated his companion. He dared not look at him.

"Well, by the time you get down there Nikopol will be gone, maybe Kishinev . . . that's as far as you'll get."

"Think so?" Andreas asked. Kishinev didn't mean anything to him either.

"Sure. Maybe even Kolomyya," laughed the man. "How long will it take you to get down there? Let's see. Tomorrow morning Breslau. Tomorrow night Przemysl. Thursday, Friday night, maybe sooner. Then: Lvov. Let's see, Saturday evening I'll be in Kolomyya; you'll need a few days longer, another week if you're smart, in a week they'll have left Nikopol, in a week Nikopol will be gone for good as far as we're concerned."

Saturday, Andreas thought. Saturday feels quite safe, no emptiness there. Saturday I'll still be alive. He hadn't dared think that close. Now he understood why his heart had been silent when he thought in months, let alone years. That had been a leap, far far beyond the goal, a shot in the void that had no echo, into the no-man's-land that no longer existed for him. It's quite close, the end is staggeringly close. Saturday. A fierce, exquisite, painful vibration. Saturday I'll still be alive, all of Saturday. Three more days. But by Saturday evening this fellow plans to be in Kolomyya, so I should be in Cernauti by late Saturday night, and it isn't going to be in Cernauti but between Lvov and Cernauti, and not Saturday. Sunday: he thought suddenly. Nothing . . . not much . . . a gentle, very, very sad and uncertain feeling. On Sunday morning I'm going to die between Lvov and Cernauti.

Now for the first time he looked at his unshaven friend. He was shocked by his face, chalk-white under the black stubble. And there was fear in the eyes. Yet he's going to a repair depot and not to the front, thought Andreas. Why this fear, why this sorrow? This was more than just a hangover. Now he looked the man straight in the eye, and he was even more shocked by that yawning abyss of despair. This was more than just fear and emptiness, something ghastly was draining him, and he knew why the man had to drink, had to drink, to pour something, anything, into that abyss. . . .

"The funny part is," the man burst out hoarsely, "the funny part is that I'm on leave. Till next Wednesday, a whole week. But I just cleared out. My wife is . . . my wife," he was choking on something terrible between a sob and rage. "My wife, you see," he said, "has got someone else. Yes," he laughed abruptly, "that's right, she's got someone else, my friend. Funny thing, you go all over Europe, sleep with a French girl here and a Rumanian whore there, and in Kiev you chase the Russian girls; and when you go on leave and stop over in some place like Warsaw or Krakow, you can't resist the pretty Polish girls either. It's impossible . . . and . . . and . . . and—" again he choked down that horrible mass of something between a sob and rage as if it were offal— "and then you get home, no warning of course, after fifteen months, and there's a guy lying on your sofa, a man, a Russian, that's right, a Russian's lying on your sofa, the phonograph's playing a tango, and your wife's sitting at the table wearing red pajamas and mixing something . . . yes that's how it was, exactly. God knows I sent home enough schnapps and liqueurs . . . from France, Hungary, Russia. The guy's so scared he half swallows his cigarette, and your wife screams like an animal . . . I tell you, like an animal!" A shudder passed over his massive shoulders. "Like an animal, I tell you, that's all I know." Andreas looked back in alarm, just one brief glance. But the blond fellow couldn't hear anything. He was calmly sitting there, quite calmly, almost comfortably, and spreading scarlet jam from an immaculate glass jar onto white bread. He spread the jam neatly and calmly, taking bites like a civil servant, almost like a chief inspector. Maybe the blond fellow was an inspector. The unshaven soldier was silent, and something made him shiver. Nobody could have heard what he said. The train had torn away his words . . . they had flown away, flown off inaudibly with the rush of air . . . maybe they had flown back to Dresden . . . to Radebeul . . . where the little fly was perched somewhere and the girl in the yellow dress was leaning against her bicycle . . . still leaning . . . still leaning. . . .

"Yes," said the unshaven soldier, speaking rapidly, almost impersonally, as if he wanted to reel off a tape he had begun. "I cleared out, simply cleared out. On the way there I had put on my work pants, I wanted to save my new black Panzer ones with the creases in them for my leave. I had been looking forward to seeing my wife . . . God, I was looking forward to it . . . not only to . . . not only to that. No, no!" He shouted: "It's something quite different, the thing you look forward to. It's at home, it's your wife, see? What you do with the other women is nothing, you've forgotten it after an hour . . . and now, now a Russian's sitting there, a tall guy, I could see that much, and the way he was lying there and smoking . . . nowhere else in the world can a man lounge around and smoke that way. Besides, I could tell by his nose he was a Russian . . . you can always tell by their noses. . . ."

I must pray more, Andreas thought, I've hardly prayed since I left home. His companion fell silent again, looking out into the gentle countryside with the sunlight lying over it like a golden shimmer. The blond fellow was still sitting there, he drank some coffee from a flask; now he was eating white bread and butter, the butter was in a brand-new container; he was eating very methodically, very neatly. I must pray more, Andreas thought, and just as he was about to begin the unshaven soldier started up again. "Yes, I cleared out. By the next train, and took the whole lot back with me. Booze and meat and money, all that money I'd taken along, everything was for her, don't you see? Why else would I have lugged all that stuff along? Just for her. What I need now is a drink . . . where can a fellow get some booze now, I've been racking my brains; these people are daft here, they don't have any black market here. . . ."

"I've got some schnapps," said Andreas, "d'you want some?"

"Schnapps . . . God, man, schnapps!"

Andreas smiled. "I'll let you have the schnapps in exchange for the map, okay?" His companion hugged him. His face was almost happy. Andreas bent over his pack and dug out a bottle of schnapps. For a moment he thought: I'll ration him, I won't give him the second bottle till he needs it or till he wakes up from the stupor he's going to drink himself into. But then he rummaged in the pack again and brought out the second bottle.

"There you are," he said, "you drink it, I don't want any!"

Soon I'm going to die, he was thinking . . . soon, soon, and this Soon was no longer quite so blurred, he had already groped his way up to this Soon, circled it and sniffed it, and already he knew that he was going to die during the night of Saturday to Sunday, between Lvov and Cernauti . . . in Galicia. Down there was Eastern Galicia, where he would be quite close to Bucovina and Volhynia. Those names were like unfamiliar drinks. Bucovina—that sounded like a sturdy plum schnapps, and Volhynia—that sounded like a very thick, swampy beer, like the beer he had once drunk in Budapest, a real soupy beer.

He glanced back once more through the glass pane and saw the unshaven soldier lifting the bottle to his mouth, and the blond fellow shake his head when the other man offered it to him. Then he looked out again but saw nothing . . . only that Polish horizon, away in the distance beyond an endless plain, that intoxicating, wide horizon that he would see when the hour came. . . .

It's a good thing I'm not alone, he thought. Nobody could go through this alone, and he was glad he had agreed to join in the game and had met these two fellows. That one who needed a shave—he had liked him from the start, and the blond fellow, well, he didn't seem as effete as he looked. Or maybe he really was effete, but he was a human being. It is not good for man to be alone. It would be terribly difficult to be alone with the others now filling up the corridor again, those fellows nattering about nothing but leave and heroism, promotions and decorations, food and tobacco and women, women, all those women who had been madly in love with every man jack of them. . . . No girl will cry over me, he thought, how strange. How sad. If only somewhere a girl would think of me! Even if she were unhappy. God is with those who are unhappy. Unhappiness is life, pain is life. It would be nice if somewhere a girl were thinking of me and crying over me . . . I would pull her after me . . . I would drag her along behind me by her tears, she shouldn't wait for me for ever and ever. There's no such girl. A strange thought. No girl I've kissed. It's just possible, though not probable, that there is one girl who still thinks of me; but she can't be thinking of me. For a tenth of a second our eyes held each other's, maybe even less than a tenth of a second, and I can't forget her eyes. For three and a half years I've had to think about them and haven't been able to forget them. Only a tenth of a second or less, and I don't know her name, I don't know a thing about her, her eyes are all I know, very gentle, almost pale, sad eyes the color of sand dark with rain; unhappy eyes, much that was animal in them and all that was human, and never, never forgotten, not for a single day in three and a half years, and I don't know her name, I don't know where she lives. Three and a half years! I don't know whether she was tall or short, I didn't even see her hands. If I had at least seen her hands! Only her face, and not even that clearly; dark hair, maybe black, maybe brown, a slender, long face, not pretty, not smooth, but the eyes, almost slanting, like dark sand, full of sorrow, and those eyes belong to me, only to me, and those eyes rested on me and smiled for a tenth of a second. . . . There was just a wall and beyond that a house, and on the wall rested two elbows, and between those elbows rested that face, rested those eyes in some French hamlet near Amiens; beneath the scorching summer sky burned gray by the heat. And there was a country road ahead of me running uphill between scrawny trees, and on the right was a wall running alongside, and behind us lay Amiens steaming as if in a cauldron; smoke hung over the town, and the murky smoke of battle smoldering like a thunderstorm; on the left motorbikes drove by with hysterical officers, tanks rumbled past on their broad tracks and showered us with dust, and somewhere up front cannon were roaring. The road going uphill suddenly made me feel giddy, it tilted before my eyes, and the wall charging madly up the hill beside the road suddenly tipped over, it simply tipped over, and I fell over with the wall, as if my life were the life of the wall. The whole world turned upside down, and all I saw of it was a plane crashing, but the plane didn't crash from above downward, from sky to ground, it crashed from ground to sky, and now I saw that the sky was the ground, I was lying on the gray-blue pitilessly hot surface of the sky. Then someone tipped brandy over my face, rubbed me, tipped some brandy down my throat, and I could raise my eyes and above me I saw the wall, that wall, that wall made of bricks with gaps in between, and on that wall rested two pointed elbows, and between the elbows I saw those eyes for a tenth of a second. Just at that moment the lieutenant shouted: "Keep going! Keep going! Get up!" And someone grabbed me by the collar and thrust me into the road, and the road pulled me away, and once again I was crammed into the column and couldn't turn around, couldn't even turn around. . . .

Is it such a disgrace, then, to long to know what forehead belonged to those eyes, what mouth and what breast and what hands? Would it have been asking too much to be allowed to know what heart belonged to them, a girl's heart perhaps; to be allowed to kiss that mouth belonging to those eyes, just once, before I got thrust into the next hamlet where all of a sudden they knocked my leg out from under me? It was summer, and the harvest stood golden in the fields, thin blades, some of them scorched black, that had been eaten up by the summer, and I hated nothing so much as to die a hero's death in a field of corn, it reminded me too much of a poem, and I didn't care to die like in a poem, to die a hero's death like a propaganda picture for this dirty war . . . and even so it was like some patriotic poem, to be lying in a field of corn, bleeding and wounded and cursing, and perhaps to have to die there, five minutes away from those eyes.

But only the bone was broken. I was a hero, wounded on the fields of France, not far from Amiens, not far from the wall that charged madly up the hill, and a mere five minutes from that face, of which I had been allowed to see only the eyes. . . .

For only a tenth of a second was I allowed to see my only love, who was perhaps no more than an apparition, and now I must die, between Lvov and Cernauti, facing the wide Polish horizon.

And didn't I promise them, those eyes, to pray for them every day, every day, and today is almost over? It's already getting dark, and yesterday I gave her only a passing thought while I was playing cards, the girl whose name I don't know and whose mouth I never kissed. . . .

It shocked Andreas to find he was suddenly hungry. It was Thursday evening, and on Sunday he was going to die, and he was hungry, he was so hungry his head ached, he was so hungry he was exhausted. It was very quiet in the corridor, and not so crowded now. He sat down beside the unshaven soldier, who promptly made room for him, and all three men were silent. Even the blond fellow was silent: he had a mouth organ between his lips and was playing it on the closed side. It was a little mouth organ, and he slid the closed side gently back and forth across his lips, and you could tell from his expression that he was hearing the tunes in his head. The unshaven soldier was drinking, drinking systematically and silently at regular intervals, and his eyes were beginning to glisten. Andreas finished the last package of air-raid sandwiches. They had got a bit dry, but his hunger welcomed them eagerly, and they tasted marvelous; he ate six whole sandwiches and asked the blond fellow for the flask of coffee. The sandwiches were really delicious, they tasted wonderful, and afterward he felt disgracefully relaxed, shockingly content. He was very glad the other two weren't talking, and the regular rattle of the train, of which they could feel the least movement, was rather soothing. Now I'll pray, he thought, I'll say all the prayers I know by heart, and a few more as well. First he said the Credo, then a Paternoster and Ave Maria, de Profundis . . . ut pupillam oculi—Come Holy Ghost; then the Credo again because it was so wonderfully complete;

then the Good Friday intercession, because it was so wonderfully all-embracing, it even included the unbelieving Jews. That made him think of Cernauti, and he said a special prayer for the Jews of Cernauti and for the Jews of Lvov, and no doubt there were Jews in Stanislav too, and in Kolomyya . . . then another Paternoster, and then a prayer of his own; it was a great place to pray, sitting beside those two silent men, one soundlessly and intently playing the wrong side of his mouth organ, the other steadily drinking schnapps. . . .

Outside it had got dark, and he prayed a long time for the eyes, a terribly long time, much longer than for all the others. And for the unshaven soldier too, and the blond fellow, and for the one who had said yesterday: Practically speaking, practically speaking we've already won the war, especially for him.

"Breslau," said the unshaven soldier suddenly, and his voice had a strangely heavy, almost metallic sound, as if he were beginning to get a bit drunk again. "Breslau, we must soon be getting into Breslau. . . ."

Andreas now recited the poem to himself: "Once there was a belfryman, in Breslau Town of old. . . ." To his mind it was a magnificent poem, and he greatly regretted not knowing quite all of it by heart. No, he thought, I'm not going to die right away. I shall die on Sunday morning or during the night, between Lvov and Cernauti, facing that immense Polish horizon.

After that he said the poem "Archibald Douglas" over to himself, thought about the sorrowful eyes, and fell asleep with a smile. . . .

Waking up was always terrible. The night before someone had stepped on his fingers, and tonight he had a terrible dream: he was sitting somewhere on a wet, very cold plain and had no legs, no legs at all, he was sitting on the stumps of his thighs, and the sky over this plain was black and lowering, and this sky was slowly sinking onto the plain, getting closer and closer, closer and closer, the sky was sinking very slowly, and he couldn't run away, and he couldn't scream because he knew it was no use screaming. The futility of it paralyzed him. Where would there be a soul hereabouts to hear his screams? Yet he couldn't let himself be crushed by that descending sky. He didn't even know whether the plain was grass, wet grass, or just earth or only mud . . . he couldn't move, he refused to hop forward on his hands like a lame bird, and where to anyway? The horizon was endless, endless, wherever he looked, and the sky was sinking, and then suddenly something very cold and wet splashed onto his head, and for a millionth of a second he thought the black sky was only rain and that it would open now, that was what he thought in the millionth of a second, and he tried to scream . . . but he awoke and instantly saw that the unshaven soldier was standing over him, the bottle raised to his mouth, and knew that a drop from the bottle had splashed onto his forehead. . . .

It all came back to him right away. Sunday morning . . . now it was Friday. Two more days. It all came back. The blond fellow was asleep, the unshaven soldier was drinking in fierce gulps, and it was cold in the compartment; there was a draft under the door, and the prayers had expired, and the thought of the eyes no longer aroused that poignant bliss, just sorrow and loneliness. It all came back, and in the morning everything looked different, everything was glamorless and everything was futile, and it would be wonderful, too wonderful for words, if in the morning this Soon could expire too, this Soon that had now become quite definite, quite certain. But this Soon was there, it was always there right away, as if it had been waiting to pounce; ever since he had uttered the word it had lain on him like second sight. For two days now it had been as close to him, as inseparably linked to him, as his soul, his heart. This Soon was just as strong and sure in the morning. Sunday morning. . . .

The unshaven soldier had also noticed that Andreas was awake. He was still standing over him, drinking from the bottle. In the dim gray light it was frightening, that bulky outline, leaning forward as if to pounce, the bottle at his lips, and the glittering eyes, and the strange, menacing gurgle from the bottle.

"Where are we?" Andreas asked in a hoarse whisper. He was scared, it was cold and still almost totally dark.

"Not far from Przemysl now," said the man. "Want a drink?"

"Yes." The schnapps tasted good. It ran into him like sharp fire, driving his blood around as fire under a kettle brings water to the boil. The schnapps tasted good, it warned him. He handed the bottle back.

"Go on, have another drink," said the man roughly. "I got myself some more in Krakow."

"No."

The man sat down beside him, and it felt good to know there was someone there who wasn't asleep, when you were awake and utterly miserable. Everyone was asleep, the blond fellow was snoring again, soft whistling sounds coming from his corner, and the others, the terribly silent and the terribly talkative, they were all asleep. The air in the corridor was foul—sour and grimy, full of sweat and steam.

Suddenly he realized they were already in Poland. His heart stood still for a moment, missed another beat as if the artery had suddenly knotted, blocking off the blood. Never again will I be in Germany, Germany's gone. The train left Germany while I was asleep. Somewhere there was a line, an invisible line across a field or right through the middle of a village, and that was the border, and the train passed callously over it, and I was no longer in Germany, and no one woke me so I could have one more look out into the night and at least see a piece of the night that hung over Germany. Of course no one knows I shan't see it again, no one knows I'm going to die, no one on the train. Never again will I see the Rhine. The Rhine! The Rhine! Never again! This train is simply taking me along, carting me off to Przemysl, and there's Poland, hopeless hapless Poland, and I'll never see the Rhine, never smell it again, that exquisite tang of water and seaweed that coats and clings to every stone along the banks of the Rhine. Never again the avenues along the Rhine, the gardens behind the villas, and the boats, so bright and clean and gay, and the bridges, those splendid bridges, spare and elegant, leaping over the water like great slender animals.

"Pass me the bottle again," he said huskily. His companion handed it to him, and he drank long and deep of that fire, that liquid fire that burns out the bleak misery of the heart. Then he lit a cigarette, and he wished his friend would say something. But first he wanted to pray, just because he felt so miserable, that was why he wanted to pray. He said the same prayers as the evening before, but this time he prayed first for the eyes, so he wouldn't forget them. The eyes were always with him, but not always with the same clarity. Sometimes they submerged for months and were only there in the sense that his lips were there and his feet, which were always with him and of which he was only occasionally aware, only when they hurt; and sometimes, at irregular intervals, often after months, the eyes would surface like some new burning pain, and on days like that he prayed in the evening for the eyes; today he had to pray for the eyes in the morning. He also prayed again for the Jews of Cernauti, and for the Jews of Stanislav and Kolomyya, there were Jews all over Galicia, Galicia, the word was like a snake with tiny feet and shaped like a knife, a snake with glittering eyes gliding smoothly over the ground and slicing, slicing the ground in two. Galicia . . . a dark, beautiful word, filled with anguish, and in this country I am going to die.

There was a lot of blood in that word, blood made to flow by the knife. Bucovina, he thought, that's a good solid word, I shan't die there, I shall die in Galicia, in Eastern Galicia. I must have a look, when it gets light, and see where the province of Bucovina begins, I won't see it any more now; I'm getting closer and closer. Cernauti is already in Bucovina, I won't see that.

"Kolomyya," he asked his companion, "is that in Galicia?"

"Don't know. Poland, I think."

Every border has a terrible finality. There's a line, and that's it. And the train goes across it just as it would go across a dead body, or a live body. And hope is dead, the hope of being sent back once more to France and finding the eyes again and the lips belonging to the eyes, and the heart and the breast, a woman's breast that must belong to those eyes. That hope is quite dead, completely cut off. For ever and ever those eyes will only be eyes, they will never surround themselves again with body and clothes and hair, no hands, no human hands, no woman's hands that might one day caress you. That hope had always been there, for after all it was a human being, a living human being, to which those eyes belonged, a girl or a woman. But not now. Now there were only eyes, no lips now, never again a mouth, a heart, never again to feel a living heart under a soft skin beating against your hand, never again . . . never . . . never. Sunday morning between Lvov and Kolomyya. Cernauti was far away now, as far as Nikopol and Kishinev. That Soon had narrowed down even more, it was very narrow now. Two days, Lvov, Kolomyya. He knew he might get barely as far as Kolomyya, but certainly no farther. No heart, no mouth, only eyes, only the soul, that unhappy lovely soul that had no body; wedged between two elbows like a witch pinned to her stake before they burn her. . . .

The border had cut off a lot of things. Paul was finally gone too. Only memory, hope, and dream. "We live on hope," Paul had once said. As if one were to say: "We live on credit." We have no security . . . nothing . . . only eyes, and don't know whether three and a half years of prayer have coaxed those eyes over to the place we may hope to reach. . . .

Yes, later on he did limp up that hill, from the hospital in Amiens, and nothing was the same. The road was not gray as it ran up the hill, it was just an ordinary road. The hill carried the road on its back, and the wall had no intention of swaying and charging; the wall just stood there. And there was the house, which he hadn't recognized, only the wall, he had recognized that, a wall made of bricks with gaps in them where bricks had been left out to make a kind of pattern. A Frenchman was standing there, a real lower-middle-class type, his pipe between his teeth, his eyes full of that truly French derision—ponderous, bourgeois—and the man had known nothing. He knew only that they had all gone, fled, and that the Germans had looted everything although a banner had been strung right across the road saying: Looting punishable by death. No, no eyes, only the man's wife, an obese matron who kept her hand tucked in the top of her dress, a face rather like a rabbit's. No child, no daughter, no sister, no sister-in-law, nothing! Just poky rooms full of kitsch and stale air and the couple's derisive looks as they watched him searching helplessly, agonizingly.

That glass cabinet: the Germans had smashed it up. And burned holes in the carpet with their cigarette butts, and slept on the couch with their whores and messed it all up. He spat with contempt. But that had all happened later, not during the battle while Amiens was smoking, much later, after the pilot had crashed in the wheatfield over there where you could see the tail of the aircraft sticking in the earth. The pipe pointed out of the window . . . yes, there it was, sticking in the earth, the tail with the emblem, and on the French steel helmet on the grave right next to it the sun was glinting; it was all real, as real as the smell from the kitchen of the roast in the oven, and the smashed glass cabinet and, down there in the valley, the cathedral in Amiens. "A fine example of French Gothic architecture. . . ."

No eyes. Nothing, nothing at all. . . .

"Maybe," said the man, "maybe it was a whore." But the man pitied him, it was a miracle that this bourgeois little man could feel pity, pity for a German soldier who belonged to the same army as the ones who had stolen his knives and forks and his clocks, and had slept on his couch with their whores, messing it all up, ruining it.

The pain was so overpowering that he just stood there in the doorway, looking at the spot on the road where he had passed out, the pain was so great that he didn't feel it. The man shook his head, perhaps he had never seen such unhappy eyes as those of this soldier leaning heavily on his cane.

"Peut-être," he said before Andreas left, "peut-être une folle, a madwoman from the asylum over there." He gestured toward the wall, where red-roofed buildings showed among fine tall trees. "A mental asylum. During the battle they all ran away, you see, and they all had to be rounded up again, a tough job. . . ."

"Thanks . . . thanks." On up the hill toward the asylum. The wall began close by, but there was no gate. It was a long, long walk up the hot hill until he reached a gate, and he knew in advance, he knew there would be no one left. A sentry in a steel helmet stood at the gate, and there were no more lunatics, only some sick and wounded and a V.D. treatment center.

"A big V.D. center," said the sentry, "did you pick up something too, bud?"

Andreas looked across to the big field where the aircraft's tail with the emblem was sticking in the earth and the steel helmet was glinting in the sun.

"It's so cheap here, that's the trouble," said the sentry, who was bored. "You can have it for fifty pfennigs," he laughed, "fifty pfennigs!"

"That's right," said Andreas . . . forty million, he thought, France has forty million inhabitants, that's too many. You can't search among all those, I must wait . . . I must look into every pair of eyes I meet. He didn't feel like walking on another three minutes and having a look at the field where he had been wounded. For it wasn't the same field, everything was different. It wasn't the same road, or the same wall, they had all forgotten; the road had forgotten too, just as people forget, and the wall had forgotten that once it had collapsed with fear and he with it. And the tail of the aircraft over there was a dream, a dream with a French emblem. Why go and look at the field? Why walk those extra three minutes and recall with hate and pain the patriotic poem that he had remembered against his will? Why torment his tired legs any further?

"Now," said the soldier who needed a shave, "now we're getting close to Przemysl." "Pass me the bottle again," said Andreas. He took another swig.

It was still cold, but dawn was softly breaking, and soon the horizon would be visible, that Polish horizon. Dark houses and a plain full of shadows, and the sky above it always threatening to collapse because there was nothing to hold it up. Perhaps this was already Galicia, perhaps this plain rising out of the dusk, drab and gray and full of sorrow and blood, perhaps this plain was already Galicia ... Galicia ... Eastern Galicia. ...

"You've had a good long sleep," said the soldier who needed a shave. "From seven to five. It's five o'clock already. Krakow to Tarnov ... all gone; I didn't sleep a wink. That's how long we've already been in Poland. Krakow to Tarnov, and now Przemysl. ..."

What a fantastic difference between Przemysl and the Rhine. I've slept for ten hours, and now I'm hungry again, and I've got forty-eight hours to live. Forty-eight hours have already gone by. For forty-eight hours this Soon has been suspended inside me: Soon I'm going to die. At first it was certain, but far off; certain, but unclear, and it's been getting steadily narrower and narrower, already it's narrowed down to a few miles of road and two days away, and every turn of these wheels brings me closer. Every turn of the wheels tears a piece off my life, off an unhappy life. These wheels are grinding away my life, whittling away my life with their stupid rhythm; they rattle across Polish soil as heedlessly as they rattled along by the Rhine, and they are the same wheels. Maybe Paul caught sight of the wheel that's under this door, this oily, dirt-encrusted train-wheel that's come all the way from Paris, maybe even from Le Havre. From Paris, the Gare Montparnasse ... soon they'll be sitting in wicker chairs under awnings and drinking wine in the autumn breeze, swallowing that sweet dust of Paris and sipping absinthe or Pernod, nonchalantly flicking their cigarette butts into the gutter that runs under that soft sky, that ever-mocking sky. There are only five million people in Paris, and many streets, many alleys, and many, many houses, and from not one of the windows do those eyes look out; even five million are too many. ...

All at once the soldier who needed a shave began speaking very rapidly. It was lighter now, and the first of the sleeping men began to stir, to turn over in their sleep, and it seemed as if he must speak before they were fully awake. He wanted to speak into the night, into a listening ear in the night. . . .

"The terrible part is that I shall never see her again, I know I won't," he said in a low voice, "and I don't know what'll become of her. It's three days now since I left, three days. What's she been doing in those three days? I don't believe that Russian is still with her—because she screamed like an animal, like an animal facing the muzzle of a hunter's gun. There's no one with her. She's waiting. God, I wouldn't want to be a woman. Always waiting . . . waiting . . . waiting . . . waiting."

The unshaven soldier screamed softly, but it was a scream all right, a terribly soft scream. "She's waiting. . . she can't live without me. There's no one with her, and no one will ever go to her now. She's waiting only for me, and I love her. Now she's as innocent as a girl that's never thought of kissing, and that innocence is all for me. That ghastly, terrible shock has completely cleansed her, I know it has . . . and no one, no one on earth can help her but me, no one, and here I am on a train heading for Przemysl . . . I'm going to Lvov to Kolomyya . . . and never again will I cross the German border. That's something no one would ever be able to understand, why I don't take the next train back to her . . . why don't I? No one would ever be able to understand that. But I'm scared of that innocence . . . and I love her very much, and I'm going to die, and all she'll ever get from me now will be an official letter saying: Fallen for Greater Germany. . . ." He took a long, deep drink.

"How slowly the train's going, mate, don't you think? I want to get away, far away . . . and quickly, and I don't know why I don't change trains and go back, I've still got time . . . I wish the train would go faster, much faster. . . ."

Some of the men had woken and were blinking morosely into the false light rising from the plain. . . .

"I'm scared," whispered the unshaven soldier into Andreas' ear,

"I'm scared, that's what, scared of dying but even more scared of going back, going back to her . . . that's why I'd rather die . . . maybe I'll write to her. . . ."

The men who had woken up were combing back their hair, lighting cigarettes, and looking contemptuously out of the windows, where dark huts stood among what seemed to be barren fields; there were no people in this country . . . somewhere over there were some hills . . . everything was gray . . . Polish horizon. . . .

The unshaven soldier was silent. There was hardly any life left in him. He had not been able to sleep all night; the spark in him had gone out, and his eyes were like blind mirrors, his cheeks yellow and cavernous, and what had been the need for a shave was now a beard, a reddish-black beard below the thick hair on his forehead.

"Those are precisely the advantages of the 37 antitank weapon," came a clipped voice, "those are precisely the advantages . . . mobility . . . mobility. . . ." "And no louder than a knock at the door," laughed an equally clipped voice.

"Not really?" "Yes, he got the Knight's Cross for that . . . and all we did was shit in our pants. . . ."

"They ought to listen to the Führer, that's what I say. Get rid of the aristocrats. Von Kruseiten he was called. What a name. A damned know-it-all. . . ." Lucky fellow, that one with the beard, asleep now when the nattering starts up and able to stay awake when everything's quiet. I must be grateful, I've still got two more nights, thought Andreas . . . two long, long nights; I'd like to be alone then. If they knew I'd prayed for the Jews in Cernauti and Stanislav and Kolomyya, they'd arrest me on the spot or stick me in the madhouse. . . . 37 antitank weapon.

The blond fellow rubbed his narrow, hideously filmy eyes for a very long time. There was something scaly in the corners of them, something disgusting, but it didn't stop him offering Andreas bread, white bread and jam. And he still had some coffee in the flask. It felt good to eat; Andreas realized he was very hungry again. It was almost a craving, and he could no longer control his eyes as they embraced the great loaf of bread. That white bread was unbelievably good.

"Yes," sighed the blond fellow, "my mother baked it for me just before I left." Later on Andreas sat for a long time in the john, smoking. The john was the only place where you could be really alone. The only place in the whole world, in the whole of Hitler's great-and-glorious army. It was good to sit there and smoke, and he felt he had once again got the better of his depression. Depression was only a bogey that haunted you just after you woke up; here he was alone, and he had everything. When he wasn't alone he had nothing. Here he had everything, Paul and the eyes of the girl he loved . . . the blond fellow and the man who needed a shave, and the one who had said: Practically speaking, practically speaking we've already won the war, and the one who had just said: Those are precisely the advantages of the 37 antitank weapon—they were all there, and the prayers were alive too, very close and warm, and it felt good to be alone. When you were alone you didn't feel so lonely any more. This evening, he thought, I'll pray for a long time again, this evening in Lvov. Lvov is the springboard . . . between Lvov and Kolomyya . . . the train was getting closer and closer to the goal, and the wheels that had rumbled through Paris, the Gare Montparnasse, maybe through Le Havre or Abbeville, were going as far as Przemysl . . . till they got quite close to the springboard. . . .

It was full daylight now, but the sun didn't seem to be coming through today; somewhere in the thick gray mass of clouds hung a pale spot with a soft gray light streaming from it that lit up the forests, distant hills . . . villages and the dark-clad figures who shaded their eyes to follow the train out of sight. Galicia . . . Galicia. . . . He stayed in the john until the deafening thumping and swearing on the other side of the door drove him out.

The train arrived in Przemysl on time. It was almost pleasant there. They waited until everyone had left the train, then woke up the man with the beard. The platform was already empty. The sun had come through and was beating down on dusty piles of rock and sand. The man with the beard knew at once what to do.

"Yes," was all he said. Then he stood up and cut the wire so they could get out right there. Andreas had the least luggage, just his pack, which was very light now that the heavy air-raid sandwiches had all been eaten. He had only a shirt and a pair of socks and some writing paper and his flask, which was always empty, and his steel helmet, since he had left his rifle behind in Paul's clothes closet where it stood propped up behind the raincoat.

The blond fellow had a Luftwaffe rucksack and a suitcase, and the bearded soldier had two cartons and a knapsack; both men also had pistols. Stepping out into the sunshine, they saw for the first time that the bearded soldier was a sergeant. The dull braid showed up now against his gray collar. The platform was deserted, the place looked like a freight yard. To the right lay army huts, hut after hut, delousing huts, cookhouse huts, recreation huts, dormitory huts, and no doubt a brothel hut where everything was guaranteed fully sanitary. Huts wherever you looked, but they walked to the left, way over to the left where there was a dead, overgrown track and an overgrown loading ramp by a fir tree. There they lay down, and in the sunshine behind the army huts they could see the old towers of Przemysl on the River San.

The bearded soldier did not sit down. He merely set his baggage on the ground and said: "I'll go and pick up our rations and find out when the train leaves for Lvov, eh? You fellows try and get some sleep." He took their leave passes and disappeared very slowly down the platform. He ambled along at a terribly slow, maddeningly slow, pace, and they saw that his blue work pants were soiled, full of stains and torn places as if from barbed wire; he walked very slowly, with almost a rolling gait, and from a distance he might have been taken for a sailor.

It was noon, very hot, and the shade of the fir tree was already drenched with heat, a dry shade without gentleness. The blond fellow had spread out his blanket, and they lay with their heads on their packs, looking toward the city across the hot steaming roofs of all those army huts. At some point the bearded soldier vanished between two huts, walking as if he didn't care where he was going. . . .

Alongside another platform stood a train about to leave for Germany. The locomotive already had steam up, and bare-headed soldiers were looking out of the windows. Why don't I get on, thought Andreas, it's really very odd. Why don't I find a seat in that train and go back to the Rhine? Why don't I buy myself a leave pass in this country where you can buy anything, and go back to Paris, the Gare Montparnasse, and comb the streets, one by one, hunt through every house and look for one little tender gesture from the hands that must belong to those eyes? Five million, that's one eighth, why shouldn't she be among them . . . why don't I go to Amiens, to the house with the pierced brick wall, and put a bullet through my head at the spot where her gaze, very close and tender, true and deep, rested in my soul for a quarter of a second? But these thoughts were as leaden as his legs. It felt great to stretch your legs, your legs got longer and longer, and he felt as though he could stretch them all the way to Przemysl.

They lay there smoking, sluggish and weary as only men can be who have been sleeping and sitting in a cramped railway car.

The sun had made a wide arc by the time Andreas awoke. The bearded soldier still was not back. The blond fellow was awake and smoking.

The train for Germany had left, but already there was another train for Germany standing there, and from the large delousing hut on the other side emerged gray figures with their parcels and knapsacks, rifles slung around their necks, bound for Germany. One of them started running, then three ran, then ten, then they were all running, bumping into one another, knocking parcels out of hands . . . and the whole gray weary wretched column of men was running because one of them had begun to panic. . . .

"Where did you put the map?" asked the blond fellow. These were the first words spoken by either of them in a long while.

Andreas pulled the map out of his tunic pocket, unfolded it, and sat up, spreading it out on his knees. His eyes went to where Galicia was, but the blond fellow's finger was lying much farther to the south and east, it was a long, shapely finger, with fine hair on it, a finger that not even the dirt had deprived of any of its good breeding.

"There," he said, "that's where I'm heading. With any luck it'll take me another ten days." His finger with its flat, still glossy, blue-sheened nail filled the whole bay between Odessa and the Crimea. The edge of the nail lay beside Nikolayev.

"Nikolayev?" Andreas asked.

"No," the blond fellow winced, and his nail slid lower down, and Andreas noticed that he was staring at the map but seeing nothing and thinking of something else. "No," said the blond fellow. "Ochakov. I'm with the antiaircraft; before that we were in Anapa, in the Kuban, you know, but we got out of there. And now it's Ochakov.

Suddenly the two men looked at one another. For the first time in the forty-eight hours they had been cooped up together, they looked at one another. They had played cards together by the hour, drunk and eaten and slept leaning against each other, but now for the first time they looked at one another. A strangely repellent, whitish-gray, slimy film coated the blond fellow's eyes. To Andreas it looked as though the man's gaze were piercing the faint first scab that closes over a festering wound. Now all at once he realized what that repulsive aura was which emanated from this man who at one time, when his eyes were still clear, must have been handsome, fair and slender with well-bred hands. So that's it, thought Andreas.

"Yes," said the blond fellow very quietly, "that's it," as if he realized what Andreas was thinking. He went on speaking, his voice quiet, uncannily quiet. "That's it. He seduced me, that sergeant major. I'm totally corrupted now, rotten to the core, life holds no more pleasure for me, not even eating, it just looked as if I enjoyed that, I eat automatically, I drink automatically, I sleep automatically. It's not my fault, they corrupted me!" he cried, then his voice subsided again.

"For six weeks we lay in a gun emplacement, way up along the Sivash River ... not a house in sight ... not even a broken wall. Marshes, water ... willow shrubs ... and the Russians flew over it when they wanted to attack our planes flying from Odessa to the Crimea. For six weeks we lay there. Words can't describe it. We were just one cannon with six men and the sergeant major. Not a living soul for miles. Our food supplies were trucked in as far as the edge of the marsh, and we had to pick them up from there and carry them across log-walks to our emplacement; the rations were always for two weeks, no shortage of grub. Eating was the only break in the monotony, that and catching fish and chasing mosquitoes ... those fantastic swarms of mosquitoes, I don't know why we didn't go out of our minds. The sergeant major was like an animal. Filth poured from his mouth all day long, those first few days, and his eating habits were foul. Meat and fat, hardly any bread." A terrible sigh was wrenched from his breast: "Any man who doesn't eat bread is a hopeless case, I tell you. Yes. . . ." Terrible silence, while the sun stood golden and warm and fair over Przemysl.

"My God," he groaned, "so he seduced us, what else is there to say? We were all like that ... except one. He refused. He was an old fellow, married and with a family; in the evening he used often to show us snapshots of his kids, and weep ... that was before. He refused, he would hit out, threaten us ... he was stronger than the five of us put together; and one night when he was alone on sentry duty, the sergeant major shot him. He crept out and put a bullet through him—from behind. With the man's own pistol; then he yanked us out of our bunks and we had to help him throw the body into the marshes. Corpses are heavy ... I'm telling you, the bodies of dead men weigh a ton. Corpses are heavier than the whole world, the six of us could scarcely carry him; it was dark and raining, and I thought: This is what hell must be like. And the sergeant major sent in a report that the old fellow had mutinied and threatened him with his weapon, and he took along the old fellow's pistol as proof—there was one bullet missing from it, of course. And they sent his wife a letter saying he had fallen for Greater Germany in the Sivash marshes . . . yes; and a week later the first food truck arrived with a telegram for me saying our factory had been destroyed and I was to go on leave; and I didn't even go back to the emplacement, I just took off!" There was a fierce joy in his voice: "I just took off! He must have hit the roof! And they first interrogated me in the office about the old fellow, and I gave them exactly the same story as the sergeant major's. And then I was off . . . off! From the battery to the section in Ochakov, then Odessa and then I took off. . . ." Terrible silence, while the sun still shone, fair and warm and gentle; Andreas felt an appalling nausea. That's the worst, he thought, that's the worst. . . .

"After that I never enjoyed anything again, and I never will. I'm scared to look at a woman. The whole time I was home I just lay around in a kind of stupor, crying away like some idiot child, and my mother thought I had some awful disease. But how could I tell her about it, it was something you can't tell anyone. . . ."

How crazy for the sun to shine like that, Andreas thought, and a dreadful nausea lay like poison in his blood. He reached for the blond fellow's hand, but the man shrank back in horror. "No," he cried, "don't!" He threw himself onto his stomach, hid his head in his arms, and sobbed. It sounded as if the ground would burst open, and above his sobbing the sky was smiling, above the army huts, above all those huts and above the towers of Przemysl on the River San. . . .

"Let me die," he sobbed, "I just want to die, then it'll be all over. Let me die. . . ." His words were stifled by a choking sound, and now Andreas could hear him crying, crying real tears, wet tears.

Andreas saw no more. A torrent of blood and dirt and slime had poured over him; he prayed, prayed desperately, as a drowning man shouts who is struggling all alone out in the middle of a lake and can see no shore and no rescuer. . . .

That's wonderful, he thought, crying is wonderful, crying is good for you, crying, crying, what wretched creature has never cried? I should cry too, that's what I should do. The sergeant cried, and the blond fellow cried, and I haven't cried for three and a half years, not one tear since I walked back down that hill into Amiens and was too lazy to walk those extra three minutes as far as the field where I had been wounded.

The second train had left too, the station was empty now. Funny, thought Andreas, even if I wanted to I couldn't go back now. I could never leave these two fellows alone. Besides, I don't want to go back, I never want to go back. . . .

The station with all its various tracks was deserted now. A heat haze danced between the rails, and somewhere back there by the entrance a group of Poles were working, shoveling ballast onto the tracks, and coming along the platform was an odd figure wearing the pants of the unshaven soldier. From way off you could see it was no longer the bearded, fierce, desperate fellow who had been cooped up in the train and drinking to drown his sorrows. This was a different person, only the pants were still those of the unshaven soldier. His face was all smooth and pink, his cap at a slight angle, and in his eyes, as he came closer, could be seen something of the real sergeant, a mixture of indifference, mockery, cynicism, and militarism. Those eyes seemed to have done with dreaming, the unshaven soldier was now shaved and washed, his hair was combed, his hands were clean, and it was just as well to know that his name was Willi, for it was impossible to think of him any more as the unshaven soldier, you had to think of him as Willi. The blond fellow was still lying on his blanket, his face on his folded arms, and from his heavy breathing you couldn't tell whether he was sleeping, groaning, or crying.

"Is he asleep?" Willi asked.

"Yes." Willi unpacked the rations and arranged everything

neatly in two piles. "Three days' supply," he said. For each man there was a whole loaf of bread and a large sausage, its wrapping paper wet with the moisture oozing from it. For each man there was slightly less than half a pound of butter, eighteen cigarettes, and three rolls of fruit drops.

"Nothing for you?" Andreas asked.

Willi looked at him in surprise, almost offended. "But I've still got my ration cards for sixteen days!" Strange to think that all that hadn't been a dream, all those things Willi had talked about during the night. It had been the truth, it had been the same person as this man facing him now, smoothly shaven, the quiet eyes holding no more than a modicum of pain; the same person who was now standing in the shade of the fir tree and, very carefully, so as not to spoil the creases, pulling on the pants of his black Panzer uniform. Brand-new pants that suited him down to the ground. He now looked every inch a sergeant.

"There's some beer here too," said Willi. He unpacked three bottles of beer, and they set up Willi's carton between them as a table and began to eat. The blond fellow did not stir, he lay there on his face as many a dead man lies on the battlefield. Willi had some Polish bacon, white bread, and onions. The beer was excellent, it was even cool.

"These Polish barbers," said Willi, "they're tremendous. For six marks, everything included, they make a new man of you, they even shampoo your hair! Just tremendous, and can they ever cut hair!" He took off his peaked cap and pointed to the well-contoured back of his head. "That's what I call a haircut." Andreas was still looking at him in amazement. In Willi's eyes there was now something sentimental, some sergeant-like sentimentality. It was very pleasant eating like this as if at a proper table, well away from those army huts.

"You fellows," said Willi, chewing and clearly enjoying his beer, "you fellows should go and have a wash, or get yourselves washed, makes you feel like a new man. You get rid of everything, all that dirt. And then the shave! You could use one." He glanced at Andreas' chin. "You could certainly use one. I tell you, it's tremendous, you don't feel tired any more, you . . . you—" he was groping for the right word—"all I can say is, you feel like a new man. You've still got time, our train doesn't leave for two hours. We'll be in Lvov this evening. From Lvov we take the civilian express, the courier train, the one that goes direct from Warsaw to Bucharest. It's a terrific train, I always take it, all you need is to get your pass stamped, and we'll see to that," he guffawed, "we'll see to that, but I'm not letting on how!"

But surely we won't need twenty-four hours to get from Lvov to that place where it's going to happen, thought Andreas. Something's wrong there. We won't be leaving Lvov as early as five tomorrow morning. The sandwiches tasted marvelous. He spread the butter thickly on the bread and ate it with chunks of the juicy sausage. That's really strange, he thought, this is Sunday's butter and maybe even part of Monday's, I'm eating butter I'm no longer entitled to. I'm not even entitled to Sunday's butter. Rations are calculated from noon to noon, and starting Sunday noon I'm not entitled to any more butter. Perhaps they'll court-martial me . . . they'll lay my body on a desk before a tribunal and say: He ate Sunday's butter and even part of Monday's, he robbed the great-and-glorious German Wehrmacht. He knew he was going to die, but that didn't stop him from eating the butter and bread and sausage and candy and from smoking the cigarettes. We can't enter that anywhere, there's no place to enter rations for the dead. We're not heathens, after all, who place food in graves for their dead. We are positive Christians, and he has robbed the positive-Christian, glorious Greater German Wehrmacht. We must find him guilty. . . .

"In Lvov," Willi laughed, "that's where I'll get that rubber stamp, in Lvov. You can get anything in Lvov, I know my way around there."

Andreas had only to say one word, only to ask, and he would have found out how and where one obtained the rubber stamp in

Lvov. Willi was just itching to tell him. But Andreas didn't care about finding out. It was fine with him if they got the stamp. The civilian express was fine with him. It was wonderful to travel by civilian train. They weren't for soldiers only, for men only. It was terrible to be always among men, men were so womanish. But in that train there would be women ... Polish women ... Rumanian women ... German women ... women spies ... diplomats' wives. It was nice to ride on a train with women ... as far as ... as ... where he was going to die. What would happen? Partisans? There were partisans all over the place, but why would partisans attack a train carrying civilians? There were plenty of leave-trains carrying whole regiments of soldiers with weapons, luggage, food, clothing, money, and ammunition.

Willi was disappointed that Andreas did not ask where he could get hold of the stamp in Lvov. He wanted so badly to talk about Lvov. "Lvov," he cried with a laugh. And since Andreas still did not ask, he launched out anyway: "In Lvov, you know, we always flogged the cars."

"Always?" Andreas was listening now. "You always flogged them?"

"I mean, when we had one to flog. We're a repair depot, see, and often there's a wreck left over, often it's a wreck that's not really a wreck at all. You just have to say it's scrap, that's all. And the superintendent has to close both eyes because he's been going to bed all the time with that Jewish girl from Cernauti. But it isn't scrap at all, that car, see? You can take two or three and make a terrific car out of them, the Russians are terrific at that. And in Lvov they'll give you forty thousand marks for it. Divided by four. Me and three men from my column. It's damn dangerous, of course, you're taking a hell of a risk." He sighed heavily. "You sweat blood, I can tell you. You never know whether the fellow you're dealing with mightn't be from the Gestapo, you can never tell, not till it's all over. For two whole weeks you sweat blood. If after two weeks there's been no report and none of the bunch have been arrested, that means you've come out on top again. Forty thousand marks." He took a drink of beer with obvious enjoyment.

"When I think of all that stuff lying in the mud around Nikopol. It's worth millions, I tell you, millions! And not a bloody soul gets a thing out of it, only the Russians. You know," he lit a cigarette, savoring it, "now and again we could flog something that wasn't so dangerous. One day a spare part, another day a motor or some tires. Clothing too. They're keen as hell to get hold of clothing. Coats, now . . . they'll fetch a thousand marks, a good coat will. Back home, you know, I've built myself a little house, a nice little house with a workshop . . . for . . . for . . . what did you say?" he asked abruptly. But Andreas had said nothing, he shot him a quick glance and saw that his eye had darkened, he was frowning, and that he hurriedly finished his beer. Even without the beard, the old face was there again . . . the sun was still shining golden above the towers of Przemysl on the River San, and the blond fellow was stirring. It was obvious he had only been pretending to be asleep. Now he was pretending to wake up. He stretched his limbs very deliberately, turned over, and opened his eyes, but he didn't know that the traces of tears in his grimy face were still plainly visible. There were proper furrows, furrows in the grime as on the face of a very little girl who has had her sandwich pinched on the playground. He didn't know this, maybe he had even forgotten that he had been crying. His eyes were red-rimmed and unsightly; he really did look as if he might have venereal disease. . . .

"Aaah," he yawned, "I'm glad there's some grub." His beer had got a bit tepid, but he gulped it down thirstily and began to eat while the other two smoked and very slowly, without the least hurry, drank vodka, crystal-clear, wonderful vodka unpacked by Willi.

"Yes," laughed Willi, but he broke off so abruptly that the other two looked at him in alarm; Willi blushed, looked at the ground, and took a big gulp of vodka.

"What was that?" Andreas asked quietly. "What were you going to say?"

Willi spoke in a very low voice. "I was going to say that I'm now drinking up our mortgage, literally our mortgage. You see, there was a mortgage on the house my wife owned when we got married, a small one of four thousand, and I had been meaning to pay it off now . . . but come on, let's drink, prost!"

The blond fellow also didn't feel like going into town to some barber, or to a washroom in one of those army huts. They tucked towels and soap under their arms, and off they went.

"And make sure your boots are nice and clean too, boys!" Willi called after them. His own boots were indeed shining with fresh polish.

Somewhere down at the end of a track there was a big water pump for the locomotives. It dripped constantly, slowly; a steady trickle of water flowed from it, and the sand all around was one large puddle. It was true, it did feel good to have a wash. If only the soap would lather properly. Andreas took his shaving soap. I shan't be needing it any more, he thought. Although it's enough for three months, of course, and it was only "issued" to me a month ago, but I shan't be needing it any more, and the partisans can have what's left. The partisans need soap too, Poles love shaving. Shaving and shoeshining are their specialties. But just as they were about to start shaving, they saw Willi in the distance calling and waving, and his gestures were so emphatic, so dramatic you might say, that they packed up their things and dried themselves off as they ran back.

"Boys!" called Willi. "There's a leave-train for Kovel just come in, it's running late, we'll be in Lvov in four hours, you can get a shave in Lvov. . . ." They slipped their tunics and coats back on again, put on their caps, and carried their luggage over to the platform where the delayed train for Kovel was standing. Not many got out at Przemysl, but Willi found a compartment from which a whole group of Panzer soldiers emerged, young fellows, boys in new uniforms that filled the air with the smell of army stores. A whole corridor became empty, and they quickly boarded the train before the ones who had stayed on it had a chance to spread themselves out with their luggage.

"Four o'clock!" cried Willi triumphantly. "That means we'll be in Lvov by ten at the very latest. That's great. Couldn't have made better time, this glorious delayed train! A whole night to ourselves, a whole night!"

They quickly installed themselves in such a way that they could at least sit back to back.

As he sat there Andreas finally managed to dry his wet ears properly; then he took everything out of his pack and neatly rearranged all the things he had hastily stuffed into it. Now there were a soiled shirt and soiled underpants and a pair of clean socks, the remains of the sausage, the remains of the butter in its container. Monday's sausage and half Monday's butter and Sunday's and Monday's candy, and cigarettes, to which he was even entitled, and even some bread left over from Sunday noon; and his prayer book, he had lugged his prayer book around all through the war and never used it. He always said his prayers just as they came to him, but he could never go on a trip without it. How strange, he thought, how strange it all is, and he lit a cigarette, one to which he was still entitled, a Saturday's cigarette, for the ration period from Friday noon to Saturday noon. . . .

The blond fellow was playing his mouth organ, and the two of them smoked in silence while the train got under way. The blond fellow was playing properly now, improvising, it seemed; soft, moving, amorphous forms that made you think of swampland.

That's it, thought Andreas, the Sivash marshes, I wonder what they're doing there now beside their cannon. He shuddered. Maybe they've killed each other off, maybe they've finished off the sergeant major, maybe they've been relieved. Let's hope they've been relieved. Tonight I'll say a prayer for the men beside the cannon in the Sivash marshes, and also for the man who fell for Greater Germany because he didn't want, because he didn't want . . . to get that way; that's truly a hero's death. His bones are lying somewhere up there in a marsh in the Crimea, no one knows where his grave is, no one's going to dig him up and take him to a heroes' cemetery, no one's ever going to think of it again, and one day he'll rise again, way up there out of the Sivash marshes, the father of two kids with a wife living in Germany, and the local Nazi leader, with a terribly sad expression, took her the letter, in Bremen or in Cologne, or in Leverkusen, maybe his wife lives in Leverkusen. He will rise again, way up there out of the Sivash marshes, and it will be revealed that he did not fall for Greater Germany at all, nor because he mutinied and attacked the sergeant major, but because he didn't want to get that way.

They were both startled when the blond fellow abruptly broke off playing; they had been swathed, wreathed about, in those soft gentle misty melodies, and now the web was torn. "Look," said the blond fellow, pointing to the arm of a soldier standing by the window and smoking a pipe, "that's what we used to make back home. Funny thing, you see so few of them, yet we used to make thousands." They didn't know what he was talking about. The blond fellow looked confused, and he blushed as he faced their puzzled eyes. "Crimea badges," he said impatiently. "We used to make lots of Crimea badges. Now they're making Kuban badges, they'll soon be handing those out. We used to make the medals for blowing up tanks too, and years ago the Sudeten medals with the tiny shield showing Hradshin Castle. In 'thirty-eight." They continued to look at him as if he were talking Greek, their eyes were still puzzled, and he reddened still further.

"For God's sake," he almost shouted, "we had a factory back home!"

"Oh," said the two others.

"Yes, a patriotic-flag factory."

"A flag factory?" Willi asked.

"Yes, that's what they called it, of course we made flags too. Truckloads of flags, I'm telling you, years ago . . . let's see . . . in 'thirty-three, I think it was. Of course, that's when it must have been. But mostly we made medals and trophies and badges for clubs, you know the sort of thing, little shields saying: 'Club Champion 1934,' or some such thing. And badges for athletic clubs and swastika pins and those little enamel flags to pin on. Red-white-and-blue, or the French vertical blue-white-and-red. We exported a lot. But since the war we've only made for ourselves. Wound badges too, huge quantities of those. Black, silver, and gold. But black, huge quantities of black. We made a lot of money. And old medals from World War I, we made those too, and combat badges, and the little ribbons you wear with civilian dress. Yes . . ." he sighed, broke off, glanced once more at the Crimea badge of the soldier who was leaning on the window and still smoking his pipe, and then he started to play again. Slowly, slowly the light bgean to fade . . . and suddenly, without transition, twilight was there, welling up stronger and darker until evening swiftly came, and you could sense the cool night on the threshold. The blond fellow went on playing his swampy melodies that wafted dreamily into them like drugs . . . Sivash, Andreas thought, I must pray for the men beside the cannon in the Sivash marshes before I go to sleep. He realized he was beginning to doze off again, his last night but one. He prayed . . . prayed . . . but the words got mixed up, everything became blurred. . . . Willie's wife in her red pajamas . . . the eyes . . . the smug little Frenchman . . . the blond fellow, and the one who had said: Practically speaking, practically speaking we've already won the war.

This time he woke up because the train stopped for a long time. At a railway station it was different, you turned over with a yawn and could feel the impatience in the wheels, and you knew the train would soon be under way. But this time the train stopped for so long that the wheels seemed frozen to the rails. The train was at a standstill. Not at a station, not on a siding. Half-asleep, Andreas groped his way to his feet and saw everyone crowding around the windows. He felt rather forlorn, all by himself like that in the dark corridor, especially since he couldn't spot Willi and the blond fellow right away. They must be up front by the windows. It was dark outside and cold, and he guessed it was at least one or two in the morning. He heard railroad cars rumbling past outside, and he heard soldiers singing in them . . . their stale, stupid, fatuous songs that were so deeply buried in their guts that they had worn a groove like a tune in a record, and as soon as they opened their mouths they sang, sang those songs: Heidemarie and Jolly Huntsman . . . . He had sung them too sometimes, without knowing or wanting to, those songs that had been sunk into them, buried in them, drilled into them so as to kill their thoughts. These were the songs they were now shouting into the dark, somber, sorrowful Polish night, and it seemed to Andreas that far off, somewhere far away he would be able to hear an echo, beyond the somber invisible horizon, a mocking, diminutive, and very distinct echo . . . Jolly Huntsman . . . Jolly Huntsman . . . Heidemarie. A lot of cars must have passed, then no more, and everyone left the windows and went back to their places. Including Willi and the blond fellow.

"The S.S.," said Willi. "They're being thrown in around Cherkassy. There's another pocket there or something. Pickpockets!"

"They'll manage it somehow," said a voice. . . .

Willi sat down beside Andreas and said it was two o'clock. "Shit, we'll miss the train at Lvov if we don't get moving right away. It's still another two hours. We'll have to leave Sunday morning. . . ."

"But we'll be starting up any minute," said the blond fellow, who was standing at the window again.

"Maybe," said Willi, "but then we won't have any time in Lvov. Half an hour is the craps for Lvov. Lvov!" He laughed.

"Me?" they suddenly heard the blond fellow call.

"Yes, you!" shouted a voice outside. "Get ready to take up your post." Grumbling, the blond fellow came back, and outside someone in a steel helmet stood on the step and stuck his face in through the train window. It was a heavy, thick skull, and they saw dark eyes and an official-looking forehead, the blond fellow having lit a match to find his belt and steel helmet.

"Any noncoms in there?" shouted the voice under the steel helmet. It was a voice that could only shout. No one spoke up. "Are there any noncoms in there, I said!"

No one spoke up. Willi gave Andreas a derisive nudge.

"Don't make me come and look for myself; if I find a noncom in there it's going to be tough for him!"

For a further second nobody spoke up, although Andreas could see that the place was swarming with noncoms. Suddenly someone quite near Andreas said: "Here!"

"Fast asleep, eh?" shouted the voice under the steel helmet.

"Yessir," said the voice, and Andreas now saw it was the man with the Crimea badge.

A few of the men laughed.

"What's your name?" shouted the voice under the steel helmet.

"Corporal Schneider."

"You'll be in charge for as long as we stop here, understand?"

"Yessir!"

"Good. You there—" he pointed to the blond fellow—"what's your name?"

"Private Siebental."

"Okay: Private Siebental will stand guard outside this car until four o'clock. If we're still here by then, have him relieved. Also, place a sentry outside the car on the other side and have him relieved too if necessary. There may be partisans in the area."

"Yessir!"

The face under the steel helmet vanished, muttering to itself: "Corporal Schneider."

Andreas was trembling. I hope to God I don't have to stand guard, he thought. I'm sitting right next to him, and he'll grab my sleeve and put me on duty. Corporal Schneider had switched on his flashlight and was shining it along the corridor. First he shone it on the collars of those who were lying down and pretending to be asleep, then he grabbed one of them by the collar, saying with a laugh: "Come on, take your gun and stand out there, and don't blame me!"

The one who had been picked swore as he got ready. I hope to God they don't find out I've no rifle, no weapon at all, that my rifle's standing propped up in Paul's closet behind his raincoat. What's Paul going to do with the rifle anyway? A chaplain with a rifle, the Gestapo'll just love that. He can't report it, because then he'd have to give my name and he would worry that they might write to my platoon. How awful that on top of everything else I had to leave my rifle behind at Paul's. . . .

"Come on, man, it's only till we get going again," said the corporal to the soldier who was cursing as he groped his way to the door and flung it open. It seemed strange that the train didn't move on; a quarter of an hour passed, they were too tense to sleep. Maybe there really were partisans in the area, and it was no joke being attacked in a train. Maybe it would be the same tomorrow night. Strange . . . strange. Maybe that's how it would be between Lvov and . . . no, not even Kolomyya. Twenty-four hours to go, twenty-four or at most twenty-six. It's already Saturday, it's actually Saturday. How utterly thoughtless I've been . . . I've known since Wednesday . . . and I've done nothing, I know it with absolute certainty, and I've hardly prayed any more than usual. I played cards. I drank. I ate and really enjoyed my food, and I slept. I slept too much, and time has leaped forward, time always leaps forward, and now here I am only twenty-four hours away from it. I've done nothing: after all, when you know you're going to die you have all kinds of things to settle, to regret, prayers to say, many prayers to say, and I've prayed hardly any more than I usually do. And yet I know for sure. I know for sure. Saturday morning. Sunday morning. Literally one more day. I must pray, pray. . . .

"Got a drink? It's lousy cold out here." The blond fellow stuck his head in through the window, and under the steel helmet his effete grayhound-head looked terrible. Willi held the bottle to the man's mouth and let him have a long drink. He also held the bottle out to Andreas.

"No," said Andreas.

"There's a train coming." It was the blond fellow's voice again. Everyone dashed to the window. It was half an hour behind the first train, and it was another of those, another troop-train, with more songs, more Jolly Huntsman . . . Jolly Huntsman and Heidemarie in that dark sorrowful Polish night. . . . Jolly Huntsman. A train like that took a long time to pass . . . with baggage car and cookhouse car and the cars for the soldiers, and all the time Jolly Huntsman and "Today it's Germany that's ours, tomorrow all the world . . . all the world . . . all the world. . . ."

"More S. S. troops," said Willi, "and all going to Cherkassy. The crap there seems to be collapsing too." He said this in an undertone, since eager and optimistic voices next to him were saying they would manage it somehow.

Softly the Jolly Huntsman died away in the night, the song growing dim in the direction of Lvov, like a subdued, very soft whimpering, and once again there was the dark sorrowful Polish night. . . .

"Let's hope there won't be another seventeen of these trains," muttered Willi. He offered Andreas the bottle again, but again Andreas refused. It's high time for me to say my prayers, he thought. This is the last night of my life but one, and I'm not going to spend it sleeping or napping. I'm not going to defile it with drink or waste it. I must say my prayers now, and above all repent. There's always so much to repent; even in an unhappy life like mine there are a lot of things to repent. That time in France when I drank a whole bottle of cherry brandy on a broiling hot day, like an animal; I keeled over like an animal, it nearly finished me. A whole bottle of cherry brandy when it was ninety in the shade, on a treeless street in some French hamlet. Because I was almost passing out with thirst and had nothing else to drink. It was ghastly, and it took me a week to get rid of my headache. And

I had a row with Paul, I always insulted him by calling him a bloody parson, I was always talking about bloody parsons. It's terrible, when you've got to die, to think you've insulted someone. I used to talk back to my teachers at school too, and I wrote Shit on the bust of Cicero; it was stupid, I was just a kid, but I knew it was wrong and silly, I did it anyway because I knew the other kids would laugh, that was the only reason I did it, because I wanted the others to laugh at a joke of mine. Out of vanity. Not because I really thought Cicero was shit; if I had done it for that reason it wouldn't have been as bad, but I did it for a joke. One should never do anything for a joke. And I used to make fun of Lieutenant Schreckmüller, of that sad, pale little fellow; the lieutenant's shoulder patches lay so heavily on his shoulders, so heavily, and you could tell he was marked for death. I used to make fun of him too, because I couldn't resist being known as a wit, as a sarcastic old trooper. That was worse than anything, maybe, and I don't know if God can forgive that. I made fun of him, of the way he looked like a Hitler Youth kid, and he was marked for death, I could tell from his face, and he was killed; he was shot down during the first attack in the Carpathians, and his body rolled down a slope, it was horrible the way it rolled down, and as the body rolled over it got covered with dirt; it was horrible, and to tell the truth it looked kind of ridiculous, that body rolling down, faster and faster, faster and faster, till it bounced onto the floor of the valley. . . .

And in Paris I abused a whore. In the middle of the night, that was awful. It was cold, and she accosted me . . . she practically assaulted me, and I could see from her fingers and the tip of her nose that she was chilled to the marrow, shivering with hunger. I felt quite sick when she said: "Come on, dearie," and I pushed her away, although she was shivering and ugly and all alone on that great wide street, and she might have been glad if I had lain beside her in her pitiful bed and just warmed her up a bit. And I actually pushed her away into the gutter and spat out abuse after her. If I only knew what became of her that night. Perhaps she drowned herself in the Seine because she was too ugly to get a nibble from anyone that night, and the terrible part is that I wouldn't have treated her so badly if she had been pretty.... If she had been pretty I might not have been so disgusted by her profession and she wouldn't have been pushed into the gutter and I might have been quite glad to warm up beside her and do some other things too. God knows what would have happened if she had been pretty. It's a terrible thing to maltreat a person because that person seems ugly to you. There are no ugly people. That poor soul. God forgive me twenty-four hours before my death for having pushed away that poor, ugly, shivering whore, at night, on that wide empty Paris street where there wasn't one single customer left for her, no one but me. God forgive me for everything, you can't undo what's done, nothing can ever be undone, and the pathetic whimpering of that poor girl will haunt that Paris street for ever and ever and accuse me, and the wretched doglike eyes of that Lieutenant Schreckmüller whose childish shoulders were not nearly strong enough for the weight of his shoulder patches. . . .

If I could only cry. I can't even cry over all these things. I feel heartsick and contrite and terrible, but I can't cry over them. Everyone else can cry, even the blond fellow, everyone but me. God grant me the power to cry. . . .

There must be a lot of other things I can't think of right now. That can't be all by a long way. There were the people I despised and loathed and mentally abused, for instance, like the man who said: Practically speaking, practically speaking we've already won the war; I hated that man too, but I forced myself to pray for him because he was such a fool. I still have to pray for the one who just said: They'll manage it somehow, and for all the ones who sang the Jolly Huntsman with such gusto.

I hated the lot of them, all those fellows who just went by in the train singing the Jolly Huntsman . . . and Heidemarie . . . and . . . A Soldier's Life is a Splendid Life . . . and . . . Today it's Germany that's ours, tomorrow all the world. I hated the lot of them, the whole lot, all those fellows who lay squashed up against me in the train and in barracks. God, those barracks. . . .

"That's it!" shouted a voice outside. "Everyone back on the train!" The blond fellow got on and the man from the other side, and the train whistled and moved off. "Thank God for that," said Willi. But it was too late anyway. It was three-thirty, and it would take them at least another two hours to get to Lvov, and the courier train, the civilian express from Warsaw to Bucharest, left at five.

"So much the better," said Willi. "That gives us a whole day in Lvov." He laughed again. He wanted so badly to tell them some more about Lvov. You could hear it in his voice, but nobody reacted, nobody asked him to go on. They were tired, it was three-thirty and cold, and the dark Polish sky hung over them, and those two battalions or regiments that were being thrown into the Cherkassy pocket had set them thinking. No one spoke, although none of them were asleep. Only the rattle of the train lulled them to sleep, killed their thoughts, sucked the thinking out of their heads, that regular clickety-clack, clickety-clack, it put them to sleep. They were all poor, gray, hungry, misguided, and deluded children, and their cradle was the trains, the leave-trains that went clickety-clack and lulled them to sleep.

The blond fellow seemed to be genuinely asleep now. He had got very cold outside, and the fug here in the corridor must have actually seemed quite warm and put him to sleep. Only Willi was awake, Willi who had once been the soldier in need of a shave. From time to time he could be heard reaching for his bottle of vodka and gulping the stuff down, swearing at intervals under his breath, and from time to time he would strike a match and smoke, and then he would light up Andreas' face and see that he was wide awake. But he said nothing. And it was odd that he should say nothing. . . .

Andreas wanted to pray, he wanted desperately to pray; first, all the prayers he had always said, and then a few more of his own, and then he wanted to say over the names, to begin to say over the names, of all the people he had to pray for, but then he thought that was crazy, to say all those names. You would have to include everybody, the whole world. You would have to say two billion names . . . forty million, he thought . . . no, two billion names it would have to be. You'd simply have to say: Everyone. But that wasn't enough, he had at least to begin to say the names of the people he had to pray for. First the ones you had hurt, the ones you were indebted to. He began with his school, then with the labor service, then the barracks and the war and all the people whose names occurred to him along the way. His uncle, he had hated him too because he had always spoken so glowingly of the army, of the happiest days of his life. He thought about his parents, whom he had never known. Paul. Paul would be getting up soon and saying mass. It will be the third he's said since I left, thought Andreas, perhaps he understood when I called out: I'm going to die . . . soon. Perhaps Paul understood and will say a mass for me Sunday morning, an hour before or after I've died. I hope Paul thinks about the others, about the soldiers who are like the blond fellow, and the ones who are like Willi, and the ones who say: Practically speaking, practically speaking we've already won the war, and the ones who day and night sing Jolly Huntsman and Heidemarie, and A Soldier's Life is a Splendid Life, and Oh, the Sun of Mexico. On this cold, miserable morning under the dark sorrowful Galician sky, he didn't think of the eyes at all. Now we must be in Galicia, he thought, quite close to Lvov, since Lvov is the capital of Galicia. Now I must be just about in the center of the net where I'm going to be caught. There's only one more province: Galicia, and I'm in Galicia. As long as I live I shall never see anything but Galicia. It has narrowed down very much, that Soon. To twenty-four hours and a few miles. Not many miles now to Lvov, maybe forty, and beyond Lvov at most another forty. My life's already been narrowed down to eighty miles in Galicia, in Galicia . . . like a knife on invisible snake's feet, a knife creeping along, softly creeping along, a softly creeping knife. Galicia. How will it happen, I wonder? Will I be shot or stabbed . . . or trampled to death . . . or will I be simply crushed to death in a crushed railway car? There are such an infinite number of ways to die. You can also be shot by a sergeant major for refusing to do what the blond fellow did; you can die any way you like, and the letter will always say: He fell for Greater Germany. And I must be sure and pray for the men with the cannon down there in the Sivash marshes . . . must be sure . . . must be sure . . . clickety-clack . . . must be sure . . . clickety-clack . . . must be sure men with cannon . . . in the Sivash marshes . . . clickety-clack. . . .

It was terrible to find he had finally fallen asleep after all. And now they were in Lvov. It was a big station, black iron girders and grimy white signboards, and there it was, in black and white, between the platforms: Lvov. This was the springboard. It was almost incredible how quickly you could get from the Rhine to Lvov. Lvov, there it was in black and white, irrevocably: Lvov. Capital of Galicia. Another forty miles less. The net was quite small now. Forty miles, maybe even less, maybe only five. Beyond Lvov, between Lvov and Cernauti, that could mean a mile beyond Lvov. Again this was as elastic as the Soon that he thought he had managed to narrow down. . . .

"Boy, can you ever sleep!" said Willi, now cheerfully collecting his belongings. "Can you ever sleep! I never saw anything like it. The train stopped twice. You nearly had to do sentry duty, but I told the corporal you were sick and he let you go on sleeping. Time to get up!" The car was empty, and the blond fellow was already standing outside with his Luftwaffe rucksack and his suitcase.

It felt very odd to be walking along a platform in the main station of Lvov. . . .

It was eleven o'clock, almost midday, and Andreas felt famished. But the thought of the sausage disgusted him. Butter and bread and something hot! It's ages since I had a hot meal, I'd like something hot to eat. Funny, he thought, as he followed Willi and the blond fellow, my first thought in Lvov is that I'd like a hot meal. Fourteen or fifteen hours before your death you feel you've got to have a hot meal. He laughed, and this made the other two turn around and look at him in surprise, but he avoided their eyes and blushed. There was the barrier, there stood a sentry in a steel helmet, as at every station in Europe, and the sentry said to Andreas, because he was the last of the three: "Waiting-room to the left, for the use of enlisted men too."

Once past the barrier Willi became almost aggressive. There he stood, in the middle of the station, lighted a cigarette, and mimicked in a loud voice: "Waiting-room for the use of enlisted men to the left! That's what they'd like, to herd us cattle into the barn they've fixed up for us." They looked at him in alarm, but he laughed. "Just leave it to me, boys. Lvov's right up my alley. Waiting-room for the use of enlisted men! There are bars in this place, restaurants," he clicked his tongue, "as good as any in Europe," and he repeated sarcastically, "as any in Europe."

His face was already beginning to look somewhat unshaven again, he seemed to have a tremendously strong growth of beard. It was the same face as before, very sad and desperate.

Without a word he preceded the others through the exit, crossed, still without a word, a big crowded square, and very quickly they found themselves in a dark narrow side street; a car was standing at the corner, a ramshackle old taxi, and, as in a dream, it turned out Willi knew the driver. "Stani," he shouted, and again as in a dream a sleepy-eyed, grubby old Pole hoisted himself in the driver's seat and recognized Willi with a grin. Willi mentioned some Polish name, and the next moment they were sitting in the taxi with their luggage, driving through Lvov. The streets were the same as in any big city anywhere in the world. Wide, elegant streets, streets that had seen better days, sad streets with faded yellow façades and looking dead and deserted. People, people, and Stani drove very fast ... as in a dream: all Lvov seemed to belong to Willi. They drove along a very wide avenue, an avenue like anywhere else in the world yet definitely a Polish avenue, and Stani came to a stop. He was given a bill, fifty marks as Andreas saw, and with a grin Stani helped them set their luggage on the sidewalk; it was all done in a few seconds, and in another few seconds they found themselves striding through a neglected front garden and entering a very long, musty hallway of a house whose façade seemed to be crumbling away. A house dating from the days of the old Hapsburg Empire. Andreas instantly recognized its aura of former Austrian Imperial grandeur; perhaps a high-ranking officer had lived here, long ago in the days of the waltz, or a senior civil servant. This was an old Austrian mansion, they could be found everywhere, all through the Balkans, in Hungary and Yugoslavia, and of course in Galicia too. All this flashed through his mind in the brief second it took to enter the long, dark, musty hallway.

But then with a happy smile Willi opened a soiled white door, very high and wide, and there was a restaurant with comfortable chairs, and attractively set tables with flowers on them, autumn flowers, thought Andreas, the kind you see on graves, and he thought: This will be my last meal before my execution. Willi led them over to an alcove that could be curtained off, and there were more comfortable chairs and an attractively set table, and it was all like a dream. Wasn't I standing a minute ago under a signboard with letters on it in black and white: Lvov?

Waiter! A smart Polish waiter wearing shiny shoes, shaved to perfection and grinning, only his jacket was a bit soiled. They all grin here, thought Andreas. The waiter's jacket was a bit soiled, but never mind, his shoes were like a grand duke's and he was shaved like a god . . . highly polished black shoes. . . .

"Georg," said Willi, "these gentlemen would like a wash and a shave." It sounded like an order. No, it was an order. Andreas had to laugh as he followed the grinning waiter. He felt as if he had been invited to the home of a genteel grandmother or a genteel uncle, and Uncle had said: Unshaven or unwashed children may not come to table. . . .

The washroom was spacious, clean. Georg brought hot water. "Perhaps the gentlemen would like some toilet soap, excellent quality, fifteen marks." "Bring it," said Andreas with a laugh, "Papa will pay for everything."

Georg brought the soap and repeated with a grin: "Papa will pay." The blond fellow had a wash too; they stripped to the waist, soaped themselves, dried themselves voluptuously, their arms and all over their yellowish-white, unaired soldiers' skin. It's lucky I brought along my socks, thought Andreas, I'll wash my feet too, and I can put on my clean socks.

Socks must be very expensive here, and why should I leave the socks in my pack? I'm sure the partisans have socks. He washed his feet and laughed at the blond fellow, who looked very astonished. The blond fellow really was in a daze.

It feels great to have a smooth chin again, as smooth as a Pole's, and I'm only sorry that tomorrow morning I'll have stubble on it again, thought Andreas. The blond fellow did not need to shave, he had only a trace of down on his upper lip. Andreas wondered for the first time how old the blond fellow might be, as he drew on his nice clean shirt, with a proper civilian collar so he could leave off that stupid army neckband; a blue shirt that had once been quite dark but was now sky-blue. He buttoned it up and drew on his tunic, his shabby gray tunic with the wound badge. Perhaps the badge was made in this fellow's patriotic-flag factory, he thought. Oh yes, he had meant to figure out the blond fellow's age. He has no beard, of course, but Paul had no beard either, and Paul is twenty-six. This fellow might be seventeen or he might be forty, he has a strange face, I expect he's twenty. Besides, he's already a private first class, he must have been serving for more than a year or almost two. Twenty—twenty-one, Andreas figured. All right. Tunic on, collar done up, it really felt great to be clean.

No thanks, they could find their way back to the alcove alone. By this time a few officers, whom they had to salute, were sitting in the restaurant. That was awful, having to salute, saluting was terrible, and it was a relief to be back in the shelter of the alcove.

"That's how I like to see you, boys," said Willi. Willi was drinking wine and smoking a cigar. The table had already been set with various plates, forks, knives, and spoons.

Georg waited on them silently. First came a soup. Bouillon, Andreas thought. He prayed softly, a long prayer; the others had already begun their soup, and he was still praying, and it was odd that they did not comment.

After the soup came some sort of potato salad, just a tiny portion. With it an aperitif. Like in France. Then came a series of meat dishes. First some meat patties . . . then something very peculiar-looking. "And what is this?" Willi asked majestically, but he laughed as he said it.

"That?" Georg grinned. "That's pork heart . . . very good pork heart. . . ." Then came a cutlet, a good juicy cutlet. A real "last meal," thought Andreas, just right for a condemned man, and he was shocked to find how good it all tasted. It's disgraceful, he thought. I ought to be praying, praying, spending the whole day somewhere on my knees, and here I am eating pork heart. . . . It's disgraceful. Next came vegetables, the first vegetables, peas. Then finally some potatoes. And then more meat, something resembling a goulash, a very tasty goulash. More vegetables, and a salad. Finally something green. And wine with everything; Willi poured, very majestically, laughing as he did so.

"We'll blow the whole mortgage today, long live the Lvov mortgage!" They drank a toast to the Lvov mortgage.

A whole series of desserts. Like in France, Andreas thought. First some creamy pudding, with real eggs in it. Then a piece of cake with hot vanilla sauce. With this they had more wine, poured by Willi, a very sweet wine. Then came something very small, a tiny object lying on a white plate. It was something with chocolate icing, puff pastry with chocolate icing and cream inside, real cream. Pity it's so small, thought Andreas. No one said a word, the blond fellow was still in a daze, it was frightening to see his face, he kept his mouth open and chewed and ate and drank. And finally there actually came some cheese. Why damn it all, exactly like in France, cheese and bread, and that was it. Cheese closes the stomach, thought Andreas; they drank white wine with it, white wine from France . . . Sauternes. . . .

My God, hadn't he drunk Sauternes in Le Treport on a terrace overlooking the sea, Sauternes, delicious as milk, fire, and honey, Sauternes in Le Treport on a terrace overlooking the sea on a summer evening, and hadn't those beloved eyes been with him that evening, almost as close as all those years ago in Amiens? Sauternes in Le Treport. It was the same wine. He had a good memory for tastes. Sauternes in Le Treport, and she had been close to him with mouth and hair and her eyes, the wine makes all this possible, and it's good to eat bread and cheese with white wine. . . .

"Well, boys," said Willi, in the best of spirits, "did you enjoy your meal?" Yes, they had really enjoyed it, they felt very content.

They had not overeaten. You must drink wine with your meal, it's wonderful. Andreas prayed . . . you must say grace after a meal, and he prayed for a long time—while the others leaned back in their chairs and smoked, Andreas propped his elbows on the table and prayed. . . .

Life is beautiful, he thought, it was beautiful. Twelve hours before my death I have to find out that life is beautiful, and it's too late. I've been ungrateful, I've denied the existence of human happiness. And life was beautiful. He turned red with humiliation, red with fear, red with remorse. I really did deny the existence of human happiness, and life was beautiful. I've had an unhappy life . . . a wasted life as they say, I've suffered every instant from this ghastly uniform, and they've nattered my ears off, and they made me shed blood on their battlefields, real blood it was, three times I was wounded on the field of so-called honor, outside Amiens, and down at Tiraspol, and then in Nikopol, and I've seen nothing but dirt and blood and shit and smelled nothing but filth . . . and misery . . . heard nothing but obscenities, and for a mere tenth of a second I was allowed to know true human love, the love of man and woman, which surely must be beautiful, for a mere tenth of a second, and twelve hours or eleven hours before my death I have to find out that life was beautiful. I drank Sauternes ... on a terrace above Le Treport by the sea, and in Cayeux, in Cayeux I also drank Sauternes, also on a summer evening, and my beloved was with me ... and in Paris I used to spend hours at those sidewalk cafés soaking up some other glorious golden wine. I know for sure my beloved was with me, and I didn't need to comb through forty million people to find happiness. I thought I had forgotten nothing, I had forgotten everything ... everything ... and this meal was wonderful. ... And the pork heart and the cheese, and the wine that gave me the power to remember that life is beautiful ... twelve hours, or eleven hours, to go. ...

Last of all he thought once more about the Jews of Cernauti, then he remembered the Jews of Lvov, and the Jews of Stanislav and Kolomyya, the cannon down there in the Sivash marshes. And the man who had said: Those are precisely the advantages of the 37 antitank weapon. ... And that poor ugly shivering whore in Paris whom he had pushed away in the night. ...

"Come on, mate, have another drink!" said Willi roughly, and Andreas raised his head and drank. There was still some wine left, the bottle was standing in the ice bucket; he emptied his glass and Willi refilled it.

All this is happening in Lvov, everything I'm doing here, he thought, in a mansion of the old Hapsburg Empire, in an old dilapidated Imperial mansion, in one of the great rooms of this house where they used to entertain on a grand scale, give glamorous balls where they danced the waltz, at least—he counted under his breath—at least twenty-eight years ago, no, twenty-nine, twenty-nine years ago there was no war yet. Twenty-nine years ago all this was still Austria ... then it was Poland ... then it was Russia ... and now, now it's all Greater Germany. They used to have balls ... they danced the waltz, wonderful waltzes, and they would smile at one another and dance ... and outdoors, in the big garden that must be behind the house, in that big garden they would kiss, the lieutenants and the girls ... and maybe the majors and the wives, and the host, he must have been a colonel or a general and he pretended not to see what was going on ... or maybe he was a very senior civil servant or some such thing ... maybe. ...

"Come on, mate, have another drink!" Yes, he'd like some more wine ... time is running out, he thought, I wonder what time it is. It was eleven, or eleven-fifteen, when we left the station, by now it must be two or three o'clock ... twelve more hours, no, more than that. The train doesn't leave till five, and then I've got till ... soon. That Soon was all blurred again now. Forty miles beyond Lvov, it won't be more than that. Forty miles, that'll be an hour and a half by train, that would make it six-thirty, it'll be light by then. All of a sudden, just as he was raising his glass to his lips, he knew it would never be light again. Thirty miles ... an hour or three quarters of an hour before the first hint of dawn. No, it'll still be dark, there'll be no dawn! That's it! That's it exactly! Five forty-five, and tomorrow is already Sunday, and tomorrow Paul begins his new week, and all this week Paul has the six o'clock mass. I shall die as Paul is mounting the steps to the altar. That's absolutely certain, when he starts reciting the antiphons without an altar boy. He once told me that you can't count on altar boys nowadays. When Paul is reciting the antiphons between Lvov and ... he must look and see which place is thirty miles beyond Lvov. He must get hold of the map. He glanced up and saw that the blond fellow was still dozing in his chair; he was tired, he had had sentry duty. Willi was awake and smiling happily, Willi was drunk, and the map was in the other man's pocket. But there was plenty of time. More than twelve hours, fifteen hours to go ... in these fifteen hours he had to see to a lot of things. Say my prayers, say my prayers, no more sleep ... whatever happened, no more sleep, and I'm glad I'm so sure now. Willi also knows he's going to die, and the blond fellow is ready to die too, their lives are over; it will soon be full, the hourglass is nearly full, and death has only a few, a very few, more grains of sand to add.

"Well, boys," said Willi, "sorry, but it's time we were moving. Nice here, wasn't it?" He nudged the blond fellow, who woke up.

He was still dreaming, his face was all dreams, and his eyes no longer had that nasty slimy look; there was something childlike about them, and that might have been because he had had a real dream, had been genuinely happy. Happiness washes away many things, just as suffering washes away many things.

"Because now," said Willi, "now we have to go to the rubber-stamp place. But I'm not giving anything away yet!" He was rather hurt that nobody asked him; he beckoned to Georg and paid something over four hundred marks. The tip was a princely one. "And a taxi," said Willi. They picked up their luggage, buckled their belts, put on their caps, and went out past the officers, past the civilians, and past the ones in the brown uniforms. And there was much amazement in the eyes of the officers and of the ones in the brown uniforms. And it was just like in every bar in Europe, in French bars, Hungarian, Rumanian, Russian, and Yugoslav bars, and Czech and Dutch and Belgian and Norwegian and Italian and Luxembourg bars: the same buckling of belts and putting on of caps and saluting at the door, as if one were leaving a temple inhabited by very stern gods.

And they left the Imperial mansion, the Imperial driveway, and Andreas cast one more glance at that crumbling façade, the waltz façade, before they got into the taxi . . . and were off.

"Now," said Willi, "now we're going to the rubber-stamp place, they open at five."

"May I have another look at the map?" Andreas asked the blond fellow, but before the latter could pull the map out of his Luftwaffe pack they were stopping again. They had driven only a short distance along the wide brooding Imperial avenue. Beyond lay open country and a few villas, and the house they had stopped at was a Polish house. The roof was flattish, the façade a dirty yellow, and the narrow tall windows were closed with shutters reminiscent of France, shutters with very narrow slits, very flimsy-looking, painted gray. It was a Polish house, this rubber-stamp place, and something told Andreas immediately that it was a brothel. The whole ground floor was hidden by a thick beech hedge, and as they walked through the front garden he saw that the ground-floor windows were not shuttered. . . .

He saw russet-colored curtains, dirty russet-colored, almost dark brown with a touch of red. "You can get any stamp in the world here," said Willi with a laugh. "You just have to know the ropes and be firm." They stood with their luggage outside the front door after Willi had pulled the bell, and it was some time before they heard any sound in the silent, mysterious house. Andreas was sure they were being watched. They were watched for a long time, so long that Willi began to get uneasy. "Damn it all," he said peevishly, "they don't have to hide anything from me. They hide everything suspicious, see, when someone they don't know comes to the door." But at that moment the door opened, and an oldish woman came toward Willi with outstretched arms and a fulsome smile.

"I almost didn't recognize you," she said in welcoming tones. "Come in! And these," she said, indicating Andreas and the other man, "these are two young friends of yours," she shook her head disapprovingly, "two very, very young friends for our house."

All three men went inside and set down their luggage in an alcove in the hall.

"We need our passes stamped for the train tomorrow morning at five, the courier train, you know the one I mean."

The woman looked doubtfully at the two younger men. She was a bit nervous. Her graying hair was a wig, you could tell. Her narrow, sharp-featured face with the gray, indeterminate eyes was made up, very discreetly made up. She was wearing a smart dress patterned in red and black, closed at the neck so as not to show her skin, that faded neck-skin, like the skin of a fowl She ought to wear a high closed collar, Andreas thought, a general's collar.

"Very well," said the woman, with some hesitation, "and . . . anything else?"

"Maybe a drink, and I'd like a girl, how about you fellows?"

"No," said Andreas, "no girl."

The blond fellow flushed and was sweating with fear. It must be terrible for him, Andreas thought, maybe it would help him to have a girl.

Suddenly Andreas heard music. It was a snatch of music, the merest shred. Somewhere a door had been opened to a room where there must be a radio, and in the half-second that the door was open he heard a few snatches of music, like someone searching along a radio panel for the right station ... jazz ... marching songs ... a resounding voice and a bit of Schubert ... Schubert ... Schubert. ... Now the door was shut again, but Andreas felt as if someone had thrust a knife into his heart and opened a secret floodgate: he turned pale, swayed, and leaned against the wall. Music ... a snatch of Schubert ... I'd give ten years of my life to hear a whole Schubert song again, but all I've got is twelve and three-quarter hours, it must be five o'clock by now.

"How about you," asked the oldish woman, whose mouth was horrible. He could see that now, it was a narrow, cramped slot of a mouth, a mouth that was only interested in money, a moneybox mouth. "How about you," asked the woman, alarmed, "don't you want anything?"

"Music," stammered Andreas, "do you sell music here too?" She looked at him in bewilderment, hesitated. No doubt there was nothing she had not sold. Rubber stamps and girls and pistols— that mouth was a mouth that dealt in everything, but she didn't know whether it was possible to sell music.

"I ..." she said, embarrassed, "music ... but of course." It's always a good idea to start with yes. You can always say no later. If you say no right off, your chances of doing business are nil.

Andreas had straightened up again. "Will you sell me some music?"

"Not without a girl," smiled the woman.

Andreas threw Willi an agonized look. He didn't know what it

would cost. Music *and* a girl, and strangely enough Willi understood that look at once. "Remember the mortgage, my lad," he
cried, "long live the Lvov mortgage! It's all ours!"

"All right," Andreas said to the woman, "I'll take some music
and a girl." The door was opened by three girls who stood laughing in the hall, they had been listening to the negotiations, two
were brunettes and one was a redhead. The redhead, who had recognized Willi and flung her arms around his neck, called out to
the oldish woman: "Why don't you sell him the 'opera singer'?"
The two brunettes laughed, and one of them appropriated the
blond fellow and laid a hand on his arm. He gave a sob at her
touch, buckled at the knees like a straw, and the brunette had to
grab him and hold on to him, whispering: "Don't be scared,
dearie, there's no need to be scared!"

Actually it was a good thing the blond fellow was sobbing; Andreas wanted to weep too, the waters behind the floodgate were
pressing forward to where the wall had been pierced. At last I'll be
able to cry, but I'm not going to cry in front of this slot of a
mouth that's only interested in money. Maybe I'll cry when I'm
with the "opera singer."

"That's right," said the remaining brunette pertly. "If he wants
music, send him the opera singer." She turned away, and Andreas,
still leaning against the wall, could hear the door being opened
again, and again his ear caught a snatch of music, but it wasn't
Schubert . . . it was something by Liszt . . . Liszt was beautiful
too . . . and Liszt could make me cry, he thought, I haven't cried
for three and a half years.

The blond fellow was leaning against his brunette like a child,
his head resting on her breast; he was weeping, and this weeping
was good. No more Sivash marshes in these tears, no more terror,
and yet much pain, much pain. And the redhead, who had a good-
natured face, said to Willi, whose arm was clasped around her
waist: "Buy him the opera singer, he's a sweetie, I think he's a real
sweetie with his music." She blew Andreas a kiss: "He's young and

a real sweetie, you old rascal, and you must buy him the opera singer and a piano. . . ."

"The mortgage, the whole Lvov mortgage is ours!" Willi shouted.

The oldish woman led Andreas up the stairs and along a corridor, past many closed doors, into a room furnished with some easy chairs, a couch, and a piano.

"This is a little bar for special occasions," she said. "The price is six hundred a night, and the opera singer—that's a nickname, of course—the opera singer costs two hundred and fifty a night, not including refreshments."

Andreas staggered over to one of the armchairs, nodded, waved her away, and was glad to see the woman go. He heard her call out in the corridor: "Olina . . . Olina. . . ."

I ought to have rented just the piano, thought Andreas, just the piano, but then he shuddered at the idea of being in this house at all. In despair he dashed to the window and flung back the curtain. Outside it was still light. Why this artificial darkness, it's the last day I'll ever see, why draw the curtains over it? The sun was still above a hill and shining with gentle warmth into gardens lying behind handsome villas, shining on the roofs of the villas. It's time they harvested the apples, Andreas thought, it's the end of September, the apples must be ripe here too. And in Cherkassy another pocket has been closed, and the pickpockets will manage it somehow. Everything's being managed, everything's being managed, and here I sit by a window in a brothel, in the "rubber-stamp house," with only twelve more hours to live, twelve and a half hours, and I ought to be praying, praying, on my knees, but I'm powerless against this floodgate that's been opened, pierced open by the dagger that was thrust into me downstairs in the hall: music. And it's just as well I'm not going to spend the whole night alone with this piano. I'd go crazy, a piano especially. A piano. It's a good thing Olina is coming, the "opera singer." The map! I forgot the map, he thought. I forgot to ask the blond fel-

low for it; I just have to know what lies thirty miles beyond
Lvov ... I just have to ... it can't be Stanislav, not even Stanislav,
I won't even get as far as Stanislav. Between Lvov and Cernauti
... how certain I was at first about Cernauti! At first I would
have been ready to bet I'd get to see Cernauti, a suburb of
Cernauti ... only another thirty miles now ... another twelve
hours. ...

He swung round in alarm at a very soft sound, as of a cat slip-
ping into the room. The opera singer was standing by the door,
which she had closed softly behind her. She was small and very
slight, with fine, delicate features, and her golden, very beautiful
hair was tied loosely back on the crown of her head. There were
red slippers on her feet, and she wore a pale-green dress. As soon
as their eyes met her hand went to her shoulder, as though to
undo her dress then and there. ...

"No!" cried Andreas, and instantly regretted letting fly at her
like that. I've already bawled out one of them, he thought, and I'll
never be able to wipe that out. The opera singer looked at him less
offended than surprised. The strange note of anguish in his voice
had caught her ear. "No," said Andreas more gently, "don't."

He moved toward her, stepped back, sat down, stood up again,
and added: "Is it all right to call you by your first name?"

"Yes," she said, very low. "My name is Olina."

"I know," he said. "Mine's Andreas."

She sat down in the armchair he gestured toward and gave him
a puzzled, almost apprehensive look. He walked to the door and
turned the key in the lock. Sitting beside her he studied her pro-
file. She had a finely drawn nose, neither round nor pointed, a Fragonard nose, he thought, and a Fragonard mouth too. She looked
wanton in a way, but she could just as easily be innocent, as inno-
cently wanton as those Fragonard shepherdesses, but she had a
Polish face, the nape of her neck was Polish, supple, elemental.

He was glad he had brought cigarettes. But he was out of
matches. She quickly got up, opened a closet that was crammed
with bottles and boxes, and took out some matches. Before hand-

ing them to him she wrote something down on a sheet of paper lying in the closet. "I have to note down everything," she said, her voice still low, "even these."

They smoked and looked out into the golden countryside with the gardens of Lvov behind the villas.

"You used to be an opera singer?" asked Andreas.

"No," she said, "they just call me that because I studied music. They think if you've studied music you must be an opera singer."

"So you can't sing?"

"Oh yes I can, but I didn't study singing, I just sing . . . like that, you know."

"And what did you study?"

"The piano," she said quietly, "I wanted to be a pianist."

How strange, thought Andreas, I wanted to be a pianist too. A stab of pain constricted his heart. I wanted to be a pianist, it was the dream of my life. I could play quite nicely, really, quite well, but school hung around my neck like a leaden weight. School prevented me. First I had to finish school. Everyone in Germany first has to finish school. You can't do a thing without a high-school diploma. First I had to finish school, and by the time I'd done that it was 1939, and I had to join the labor service, and by the time I was through with that the war had started; that was four and a half years ago and I haven't touched a piano since. I wanted to be a pianist. I dreamed about it, just as much as other people dream of becoming school principals. But I wanted to be a pianist, and I loved the piano more than anything else in the world, but nothing came of it. First school, then labor service, and by that time they'd started a war, the bastards. . . . The pain was suffocating him, and he had never felt as wretched in his life. It'll do me good to suffer. Perhaps that'll help me to be forgiven for sitting here in a brothel in Lvov beside the opera singer who costs two hundred and fifty for a whole night without matches and without piano, the piano that costs six hundred. Perhaps I'll be forgiven for all that because this pain is numbing me, paralyzing me, because she said the words "pianist" and "piano." It's excruciating, this pain, it's like an acrid poison in my throat and it's sliding farther and farther down, through my gullet and into my stomach and spreading all through my body. Half an hour ago I was still happy because I'd drunk Sauternes, because I remembered the terrace above Le Treport where the eyes had been very close to me, and where I played the piano to them, to those eyes, in my imagination, and now I'm consumed with agony, sitting in this brothel beside this lovely girl whom the entire great-and-glorious German Wehrmacht would envy me. And I'm glad I'm suffering, I'm glad I'm almost passing out with pain, I'm happy to be suffering, suffering so excruciatingly, because then I may hope to be forgiven everything, forgiven for not praying, praying, praying, not spending my last twelve hours on my knees praying. But where could I kneel? Nowhere on earth could I kneel in peace. I'll tell Olina to keep watch at the door, and I'll get Willi to pay six hundred marks for the piano, and two hundred and fifty marks for the beautiful opera singer without matches, and I'll buy Olina a bottle of wine so she won't get bored. . . .

"What's the matter?" Olina asked. There was surprise in her gentle voice since he had cried no.

He looked at her, and it was wonderful to see her eyes. Gray, very gentle, sad eyes. He must give her an answer.

"Nothing," he said; and then suddenly he asked, and it was a tremendous effort to force the few words out of his mouth through the poison of his pain: "Did you finish your music studies?"

"No," she said shortly, and he saw it would be cruel to question her. She tossed her cigarette into the large metal ashtray that she had placed on the floor between their two armchairs, and asked, her voice low and gentle again: "Shall I tell you about it?"

"Yes," he said, not daring to look at her, for those gray eyes, that were perfectly calm, scared him.

"All right." But she did not begin. She was looking at the floor; he was aware when she raised her head, then she asked suddenly: "How old are you?"

"In February I would be twenty-four," he said quietly.

"In February you would be twenty-four. Would be . . . won't you be?"

He looked at her, astonished. What a sensitive ear she had! And all at once he knew he would tell her about it, her alone. She was the only person who was to know everything, that he was going to die, tomorrow morning, just before six, or just after six, in. . . .

"Oh well," he said, "it's just a manner of speaking. What's the place called," he asked suddenly, "that lies thirty miles beyond Lvov toward . . . toward Cernauti?"

Her astonishment was growing. "Stryy," she said.

Stryy? What a strange name, Andreas thought, I must have overlooked it on the map. For God's sake, I must pray for the Jews of Stryy too. Let's hope there are still some Jews in Stryy . . . Stryy . . . so that's where it will be, he would die just this side of Stryy . . . not even Stanislav, not even Kolomyya, and a long long way this side of Cernauti. Stryy! That was it! Maybe it wasn't even on that map of Willi's. . . .

"So you'll be twenty-four in February," said Olina. "Funny, so will I." He looked at her. She smiled. "So will I," she repeated. "I was born February 12, 1920."

They looked at each other for a long time, a very long time, and their eyes sank into one another's, and then Olina leaned toward him, and because the chairs were too far apart she rose, moved toward him, and made as if to put her arms around him, but he turned aside. "No," he said quietly, "not that, don't be angry with me, later . . . I'll explain. . . . My . . . my birthday's February 15."

She lit another cigarette, he was glad he hadn't offended her. She was smiling. She was thinking, after all he's hired the room and me for the whole night. And it's only six o'clock, not even quite six. . . .

"You were going to tell me about it," said Andreas.

"Yes," she said. "We're the same age, I like that. I'm three days older than you. I expect I'm your sister. . . ." She laughed. "Maybe I really am your sister."

"Please tell me about it."

"I am," she said, "I am telling you. In Warsaw I studied at the Conservatory of Music. You wanted to hear about my studies, didn't you?"

"Yes!"

"Do you know Warsaw?"

"No."

"Well then. Here we go. Warsaw is a big city, a beautiful city, and the Conservatory was in a house like this one. Only the garden was bigger, much bigger. During recess we could stroll in that lovely big garden and flirt. They told me I was very talented. I took piano. I would rather have played only the harpsichord at first, but no one taught that, so I had to take piano. For my entrance test I had to play a short, simple little Beethoven sonata. That was tricky. It's so easy to make a mess of those simple little things, or one plays them too emotionally. It's very difficult to play those simple things. It was Beethoven, you know, but a very early Beethoven, almost classical in style, almost like Haydn. A very subtle piece for an entrance test, d'you see?"

"Yes," said Andreas, and he could sense that soon he was going to cry.

"Good. I passed, with Very Good. I studied and played till . . . let's see . . . till the war started. That's right, it was the fall of 'thirty-nine, two years; I learned a lot and flirted a lot. I always did like kissing and all that, you know. I could play Liszt quite well by that time, and Tchaikovsky. But I could never really play Bach properly. I would have liked to play Bach. And I could play Chopin quite well too. Fine. Then came the war. . . . Oh yes, and there was a garden behind the Conservatory, a wonderful garden, with benches and arbors, and sometimes we had parties, and there would be music and dancing in the garden. Once we had a Mozart evening, a wonderful Mozart evening. . . . Mozart was another one I could already play quite well. Well, then came the war!"

She broke off abruptly, and Andreas turned questioning eyes on her. She looked angry. The hair seemed to bristle above that Fragonard forehead.

"For God's sake," she burst out, "do what the others all do with me. This is ridiculous!"

"No," said Andreas, "you have to tell me."

"That," she said frowning, "is something you can't pay for."

"Yes I can," he said, "I'll pay in the same coin. I'll tell you my story too. Everything. . . ."

But she was silent. She stared at the floor and was silent. He studied her out of the corner of his eye and thought: she does look like a tart after all. There's sex in every fiber of that pretty face, and she's not an innocent shepherdess, she's a very wanton shepherdess. It gave him a pang to find that she was a tart after all. The dream had been very lovely. She might be standing anywhere in the Gare Montparnasse. And it did him good to feel that pain again. For a time it had completely gone. He loved listening to her gentle voice telling him about the Conservatory. . . .

"It's boring," she said suddenly. She spoke with complete indifference.

"Let's have some wine," said Andreas.

She rose, walked briskly to the closet, and in a businesslike voice asked: "What would you like to drink?" She looked into the closet: "There's some red wine and some white, Moselle, I think."

"All right," he said, "let's have some Moselle."

She brought over the bottle, pushed a little table up to their chairs, handed him the corkscrew, and set out glasses while he opened the bottle. He watched her, then poured the wine, they raised their glasses, and he smiled into her angry eyes.

"Let's drink to the year of our birth," he said, "1920."

She smiled against her will. "All right, but I'm not going to tell you any more."

"Shall I tell you my story?"

"No," she said. "All you fellows can talk about is the war. I've been listening to that for two years now. Always the war. As soon as you've finished . . . you begin talking about the war. It's boring."

"What would you like to do then?"

"I'd like to seduce you, you're a virgin, aren't you?"

"Yes," said Andreas, and was taken aback at the way she promptly jumped up. "I knew it," she cried, "I knew it!" He saw her eager, flushed face, the eyes flashing at him, and thought: Funny, I've never seen any woman I've desired less than this one, and she's beautiful, and I could have her right now. Oh yes, sometimes a thrill has gone through me, without my trying or wanting it, and for that split second I've known that it must be truly wonderful to possess a woman. But there's never been one I desired as little as this one. I'll tell her about it, I'll tell her everything. . . .

"Olina," he said, pointing to the piano, "Olina, play the little Beethoven sonata."

"Promise you'll . . . promise you'll make love to me."

"No," he said quietly. "Come and sit here." He made her sit beside him in the armchair, and she looked at him without saying a word.

"Now listen," he said, "I'm going to tell you my story."

He looked out of the window and saw that the sun had gone down and that only a very little light remained over the gardens. Very soon there would be no more sunlight outside in the gardens, and never again, never again would the sun shine, never again would he see a single ray of sunshine. The last night was beginning, and the last day had passed like all the others, wasted and meaningless. He had prayed a bit and drunk some wine and now he was in a brothel. He waited until it was dark. He had no idea how long it took, he had forgotten the girl, forgotten the wine, the whole house, and all he saw was a last little bit of the forest whose treetops caught a few final glints from the setting sun, a few tiny glints from the sun. Some reddish gleams, exquisite, indescribably beautiful on those treetops. A tiny crown of light, the last light he would ever see. Now it was gone . . . no, there was still a bit, a tiny little bit on the tallest of the trees, the one that reached up the highest and could still catch something of the golden reflection that would remain for only half a second ... until it was all gone. It's still there, he thought, holding his breath ... still a particle of light up there on the treetop ... an absurd little shimmer of sunlight, and no one in the world but me is watching it. Still there ... still there, it was like a smile that faded very slowly ... still there, and now it was gone! The light has gone out, the lantern has vanished, and I shall never see it again. ...

"Olina," he said softly, and he felt he could speak now, and he knew he would win her because it was dark. A woman can only be won in the dark. Funny, he thought, I wonder if that's really true? He had the feeling that Olina belonged to him now, had surrendered to him. "Olina," he said softly, "tomorrow morning I must die. That's right," he said calmly, looking at her shocked face, "don't be scared! Tomorrow morning I must die. You're the first and only person I've told. I am certain. I must die. A moment ago the sun went down. Just this side of Stryy I shall die. ..."

She jumped to her feet and looked at him in horror. "You're mad," she whispered, white-faced.

"No," he said, "I'm not mad, that's how it is, you must believe me. You must believe that I'm not mad, that tomorrow morning I shall die, and now you must play me the little Beethoven sonata."

She stared at him, aghast, and murmured: "But ... but that's impossible."

"I'm absolutely certain and you have told me the last thing I needed to know, Stryy, that's it. What a terrible name, Stryy. What kind of a word is that? Stryy? Why must I die just this side of Stryy? Why did it have first to be between Lvov and Cernauti ... then Kolomyya ... then Stanislav ... then Stryy. The moment you said Stryy I knew that was the place. Wait!" he called, as she rushed to the door and stood staring at him with terrified eyes.

"You must stay with me," he said, "you must stay with me. I'm a human being, and I can't stand it alone. Stay with me, Olina. I'm not mad. Don't scream." He held his hand over her mouth. "My God, what can I do to prove to you I'm not mad? What can I do? Tell me what I can do to prove to you I'm not mad?"

But she was too frightened to hear what he was saying. She merely stared at him with her terrified eyes, and all at once he realized what a dreadful profession she had. If he were really mad, she would now be standing there helpless. They send her to a room, and two hundred and fifty marks are paid for her because she is the "opera singer," a very valuable little doll, and she has to go to that room like a soldier going to the front. She has to go, even though she is the opera singer, a very valuable little doll. A terrible life. They send her to a room and she has no idea who is inside. An old man, a young one, an ugly man or a handsome one, bestial or innocent. She has no idea and goes to the room, and now there she is, frightened, just frightened, too frightened to hear what he is saying. It is truly a sin to go to a brothel, he thought. They send girls to a room, just like that.... He gently stroked the hand he was restraining her by, and strangely enough the fear in her eyes began to recede. He went on stroking it, and felt as if he were stroking a child. I've never desired a woman as little as this one. A child ... and suddenly he saw that poor grubby little girl in a suburb of Berlin, playing among prefabs where there were some scrawny gardens, and the other kids had taken her doll and thrown it into a puddle ... and then run away. And he had bent down and pulled the doll out of the puddle; it was dripping with dirty water, a dangling, frayed, cheap ragdoll, and he had to stroke the child for a long time and try and console her for her poor doll having got wet ... a child. ...

"You're all right now, aren't you?" he said. She nodded, and there were tears in her eyes. He led her gently back to the chair. The dusk had become heavy and sad.

She sat down obediently, keeping her still somewhat nervous gaze on him. He poured her some wine. She drank. Then she sighed deeply. "God, how you scared me," she said, and thirstily gulped down the rest of her wine.

"Olina," he said, "you're twenty-three now. Just ask yourself whether you're going to be twenty-five, will you?" he urged her. "Say to yourself: I am twenty-five years old. That's February 1945,

Olina. Try, think hard." She closed her eyes, and he saw from her lips that she was saying something under her breath that in Polish must mean: February 1945.

"No," she said, as if waking up, and she shook her head. "There's nothing there, as if it didn't exist—how odd."

"You see?" he said. "And when I think: Sunday noon, tomorrow noon, that doesn't exist for me. That's the way it is. I'm not mad." He saw her close her eyes again and say something under her breath. . . .

"It's odd," she said softly, "but February 1944 doesn't exist either. . . ."

"Oh for heaven's sake," she broke out, "why won't you make love? Why won't you dance with me?" She moved swiftly to the piano and sat down. And then she played: "I'm dancing with you into heaven, the seventh heaven of love. . . ."

Andreas smiled. "Come on, play the Beethoven sonata . . . play a. . . ."

But again she was playing: I'm dancing with you into heaven, the seventh heaven of love. She played it very softly, as softly as dusk was now sinking into the room through the open curtains. She played the sentimental tune unsentimentally, which was strange. The notes sounded crisp, almost staccato, very soft, almost as if suddenly she were turning this brothel piano into a harpsichord. Harpsichord, thought Andreas, that's the right instrument for her, she ought to play the harpsichord. . . .

The popular tune she was now playing was no longer the same, yet it was the same. What a lovely tune it is, thought Andreas. It's fantastic, what she can make of it. Perhaps she studied composition too, and she's turning this trivial tune into a sonata hovering in the dusk. Now and again, at intervals, she would play the original melody again, pure and clear, unsentimentally: I'm dancing with you into heaven, the seventh heaven of love. Now and again, between the gentle, playful waves, she allowed the theme to rear up like a granite cliff.

It was almost dark now, it was getting chilly, but he didn't care; the music sounded so beautiful that he wasn't going to get up and close the window; even if subzero air were to come in through the window from the gardens of Lvov, he wasn't going to get up. . . . Maybe I'm dreaming it's 1943 and I'm sitting here in a Lvov brothel wearing the gray tunic of Hitler's army; maybe I'm dreaming, maybe I was born in the seventeenth century or the eighteenth, and I'm sitting in my mistress's drawing-room, and she's playing the harpsichord, just for me, all the music in the world just for me . . . in a chateau somewhere in France, or a little schloss in western Germany, and I'm listening to the harpsichord in an eighteenth-century drawing-room, played by someone who loves me, who is playing just for me, just for me. The whole world is mine, here in the dusk; very soon the candles will be lit, we won't call a servant . . . no, no servant . . . I shall light the candles with a paper spill, and I shall light the paper spill with my pay-book from the fire in the hearth. No, there's no fire burning in the hearth. I shall light the fire myself, the air from the garden, from the grounds of the chateau, is damp and cool; I shall kneel by the hearth, tenderly place the kindling in layers, crumple each page of my paybook, and light the fire with the matches she noted down. Those matches will be paid for with the Lvov mortgage. I shall kneel at her feet, for she will be waiting with tender impatience for the fire to be lit in the hearth. Her feet have grown cold at the harpsichord; she has sat at the open window in this damp, cool air for a long, long time, playing for me, my sister, she has been play-ing so beautifully that I wouldn't get up to close the window . . . and I shall make a lovely bright fire, and we won't need any ser-vants, no indeed, no servants! Just as well the door is locked. . . .

1943. A terrible century; what awful clothes the men will be wearing; they will glorify war and wear dirt-colored clothes in the war, while we never glorified war, war was an honest craft at which now and again a man got cheated of his rightful wages; and we wore cheerful clothes when we worked at this craft, just as a doctor wears cheerful clothes and a mayor . . . and a prostitute; but those people will be wearing horrible clothes and will glorify war and fight wars for their national honor: a terrible century; 1943. . . .

We have all night, all night. Dusk has only just fallen in the garden, the door is locked, and nothing can disturb us; the whole chateau is ours; wine and candles and a harpsichord! Eight hundred and fifty marks without the matches; millions lying around Nikopol! Nikopol! Nothing! . . . Kishinev? Nothing! . . . Cernauti? Nothing! . . . Kolomyya? Nothing! . . . Stanislav? Nothing! Stryy . . . Stryy . . . that terrible name that is like a streak, a bloody streak across my throat! In Stryy I'm going to be murdered. Every death is a murder, every death in war is a murder for which someone is responsible. In Stryy!

I'm dancing with you into heaven, the seventh heaven of love!

It was not a dream at all, a dream ending with the last note of that melodic paraphrase, it merely tore the frail web that had been cast over him, and now for the first time, by the open window, in the cool of the dusk, he realized he had been crying. He had neither known it nor felt it, but his face was wet, and Olina's hands, soft and very small, were drying his face; the rivulets had run down his face and collected in the closed collar of his tunic; she undid the hook and dried his neck with her handkerchief. She dried his cheeks and around his eyes, and he was grateful that she said nothing. . . .

A strangely sober joy filled him. The girl switched on the light, closed the window with averted face, and it was possible she had been crying too. This chaste happiness is something I have never known, he thought, as she crossed to the closet. I've always only desired, I've desired an unknown body, and I've desired that soul too, but here I desire nothing. . . . How strange that I have to find this out in a Lvov brothel, on the last evening of my life, on the threshold of the last night of my earthly existence that is to come to an end tomorrow morning in Stryy with a bloody streak. . . .

"Lie down," said Olina. She indicated the little sofa, and he noticed that she had switched on an electric kettle in that mysterious closet.

"I'll make some coffee," she said, "and until it's ready I'll go on with my story."

He lay down, and she sat beside him. They smoked, the ashtray lying conveniently on a stool so they could both reach it. He barely needed to stretch out his hand.

"I needn't tell you," she began quietly, "that you musn't ever speak to anyone about it. Even if you . . . if you were not to die—you would never betray my secret. I know that. I had to swear by God and all the saints and by our beloved Poland that I would never tell a soul, but if I tell you it's as if I were telling myself, and I can't keep anything from you any more than I can keep anything from myself!" She stood up and poured the bubbling water very slowly and tenderly into a small coffeepot. Each time she paused for a few seconds she would smile at him before continuing to pour, very slowly, and now he could see she had been crying too. Then she filled the cups that were standing beside the ashtray.

"The war broke out in 1939. In Warsaw my parents were buried under the ruins of our big house, and there I was all alone in the garden of the Conservatory, where I had been flirting, and the director was taken away because he was a Jew. Well, I just didn't feel like going on with the piano. The Germans had somehow or other raped us all, every single one of us." She drank some coffee, he took a sip too. She smiled at him.

"It's funny that you're a German and I don't hate you." She fell silent again, smiling, and he thought, it's remarkable how quickly she's surrendered. When she went to the piano she wanted to seduce me, and the first time she played I'm dancing with you into heaven, the seventh heaven of love, it was still far from clear. While she was playing she cried. . . .

"All Poland," she went on, "is a resistance movement. You people have no idea. No one suspects how big it is. There is hardly a single unpatriotic Pole. When one of you Germans sells his pistol anywhere in Warsaw or Krakow, he should realize that in doing so he's selling as many of his comrades' lives as there is ammunition in that pistol. When anywhere, anywhere at all," she went on passionately, "a general or a lance-corporal sleeps with a girl and so much as tells her they didn't get any rations near Kiev or Kishinev or some such place, or that they retreated only two miles, he never suspects that this is jotted down, and that this gladdens the girl's heart more than the twenty or two hundred and fifty zlotys she's been paid for her seeming surrender. It's so easy to be a spy among you people that I soon got disgusted with it. All one had to do was get on with it. I don't understand it."

She shook her head and gave him a look almost of contempt.

"I don't understand it. You're the most garrulous people in the world, and sentimental down to your fingertips. Which army are you with?"

He told her the number.

"No," she said, "he was from a different one. A general who used to come and see me here sometimes. He talked like a sentimental schoolboy who's had a bit too much to drink. 'My boys,' he would groan, 'my poor boys!' And a little later on the old lecher would be babbling away to me about all kinds of things that were vitally important. He's got a lot of his poor boys on his conscience ... and he told me a lot of things. And then ... then," she hesitated, "then I'd be like ice. . . ."

"And were there some you loved?" asked Andreas. Funny, he thought, that it should hurt to know there were some she might have loved.

"Yes," she said, "there were some I really loved, not many." She looked at him, and he saw she was crying again. He took her hand, sat up, and poured coffee with his free hand.

"Soldiers," she said softly. "Yes. There were some soldiers I loved ... and I knew it made no difference that they were Germans whom actually I ought to have hated. You know, when I gave myself to them I felt I was no longer part of the terrible game we're all playing, the game I had an especially big part in. The game of sending others to their death, men one didn't know. You see," she whispered, "some fellow, a lance-corporal or a general, tells me something here, and I pass on the information—machinery is set in motion, and somewhere men die because I passed on that information, do you see what I mean?" She looked at him out of frantic eyes. "Do you see what I mean? Or take yourself: you tell some fellow at the station: Take that train, bud, rather than that one—and that's the very train the partisans attack, and your buddy dies because you told him: Take that train. That's why it was so wonderful just to give oneself to them, just abandon oneself, and forget everything else. I asked them nothing for our mosaic and told them nothing, I had to love them. And what's so terrible is that afterwards they're always sad. . . ."

"Mosaic," asked Andreas huskily, "what's that?"

"The whole espionage system is a mosaic. Everything's assembled and numbered, every smallest scrap we get hold of, until the picture's complete . . . it slowly fills out . . . and many of these mosaics make up the whole picture . . . of you people . . . of your war . . . your army. . . ."

"You know," she went on, looking at him very seriously, "the terrible part is that it's all so senseless. Everywhere it's only the innocent who are murdered. Everywhere. By us too. Somehow I've always known that—" she looked away from him—"but, you know what frightens me is that I didn't grasp it fully till I walked into this room and saw you. Your shoulders, the back of your neck, there in the golden sunshine." She pointed to the window where the two chairs were.

"I know that now. When they sent me here, when Madame told me: 'There's someone waiting for you in the bar, I don't think you'll get much out of him but at least he pays well'—as soon as she said that I thought: I'll get something out of him all right. Or it's someone I can love. Not one of the victims, because there are only victims and executioners. And when I saw you standing over there by the window, your shoulders, the back of your neck, your stooping young figure as if you were thousands of years old, it came to me for the first time that we also only murder the innocent . . . only the innocent. . . ."

The soundlessness of that crying was terrible. Andreas rose, stroked the nape of her neck in passing, and went to the piano. Her eyes followed him in astonishment. Her tears dried up at once, she watched him as he sat there, on the piano stool, staring at the keys, his hands spread apprehensively, and across his forehead there was a terrible furrow, an anguished furrow.

He's forgotten me, she thought, he's forgotten me, how awful it is that they always forget us at the very moment when they are really themselves. He's not thinking about me any more, he'll never think about me any more. Tomorrow morning he will die in Stryy . . . and he'll waste no more thoughts on me.

He is the first and only one I've loved. The first. He is absolutely alone now. He is unbelievably sad and alone. That furrow across his forehead, it cuts him in two, his face is pale with terror, and he has spread his hands as if he had to grasp some dreadful animal. . . . If he could only play, if he could only play, he would be with me again. The first note will give him back to me. To me, to me, he belongs to me . . . he is my brother, I am three days older than he is. If he could only play. There's some monstrous cramp inside him, spreading his hands, turning him deathly pale, making him fearfully unhappy. There's nothing left of all I wanted to give him with my playing . . . with my story, there's nothing of all that with him now. It's all gone, he's alone now with his pain.

And indeed, when all at once he attacked the keys with a fierce rage in his face, he raised his eyes, and his eyes went straight to her. He smiled at her, and she had never seen such a happy face as that face of his above the black surface of the piano in the soft yellow lamplight. Oh how I love him, she thought. How happy he is, he's mine, here in this room till morning. . . .

She had imagined he would play something crazy, some wild piece by Tchaikovsky or Liszt or one of those glorious lilting Chopin pieces, because he had attacked the keys like a madman.

No, he played a sonatina by Beethoven. A delicate little piece, very tricky, and for a second she was afraid he would "mess it up." But he played very beautifully, very carefully, perhaps a shade too carefully, as if he did not trust his own strength. How tenderly he played, and she had never seen such a happy face as that soldier's face above the polished surface of the piano. He played the sonatina a little uncertainly, but purely, more purely than she had ever heard it, very clear and clean.

She hoped he would go on playing. It was wonderful; she had lain down on the sofa, where he had been lying, and she saw the cigarette gradually burning away in the ashtray: she longed to draw on it but dared not move; the slightest movement might destroy that music; and the best part of all was that very happy soldier's face above the black, shining surface of the piano. . . .

"No," he said with a laugh as he got to his feet. "There's not much left. It's no use. The fact is, you have to have studied, and I never did." He bent over her and dried her tears, and he was glad she had cried. "No," he said softly, "stay where you are. I was going to tell you my story too, remember?"

"Yes," she whispered. "Tell me, and give me some wine."

This is happiness, he thought, as he went to the closet. This is bliss, although I've just discovered that I'm no good at the piano. There's been no miracle. I haven't suddenly become a pianist. It's done with now, and yet I'm happy. He looked into the closet and asked over his shoulder: "Which would you like?"

"Red," she said with a smile, "a red one now."

He took a less slender bottle out of the closet, then he saw the sheet of paper and the pencil and studied the paper. At the top was something in Polish: that would be the matches; then came "Mosel" in German, and in front of that a Polish word no doubt meaning bottle. What charming handwriting she has, he thought, pretty, feminine handwriting, and under "Mosel" he wrote "Bordeaux," and below the Polish word for bottle he made two dots. "Did you really put it down?" she asked, smiling, as he poured the wine.

"Yes."

"You wouldn't even cheat a madame."

"Yes I would," he said, and he suddenly remembered Dresden

station, and the taste of Dresden station, painfully distinct, was in his mouth, and he saw the fat, red-faced lieutenant. "Yes I would, I once tricked a lieutenant." He told her the story. She laughed. "But that isn't so bad."

"Yes it is," he said, "it's very bad. I shouldn't have done that, I should have called out after him: I'm not deaf. I said nothing, because I have to die soon and because he yelled at me like that ... because I was full of pain. Besides, I was too lazy. Yes," he said softly, "I actually was too lazy to do it because it was so wonderful to have the taste of life in my mouth. I wanted to get it clear, I remember exactly, I thought: You must never let someone feel humiliated on your account, even if it's a brand-new lieutenant, not even if he has brand-new medals on his chest. You must never let that happen, I thought, and I can still see him walking off, embarrassed and smarting, crimson in the face, followed by his grinning flock of subordinates. I can see his fat arms and his pathetic shoulders. When I think of those pathetic, stupid shoulders of his I almost have to weep. But I was too lazy, just too lazy, to open my mouth. It wasn't even fear, just plain laziness. God, I thought, how beautiful life is after all, all these people milling about on the platform. One's going to his wife, the other to his girl, and that woman's going to her son, and it's autumn, how wonderful, and that couple over there going toward the barrier, this evening or tonight they'll be kissing under the soft trees down by the Elbe." He sighed. "I'll tell you all the people I've cheated!"

"Oh no," she said, "don't. Tell me something nice ... and pour me some more!" She laughed. "Who could you ever have cheated?"

"I'll tell you the truth. Everything I've stolen and all the people I've cheated...." He poured more wine, they raised their glasses, and in that second while they looked at each other, smiling, over the rims of their glasses, he drew her lovely face deep within himself. I mustn't lose it, he thought, I must never lose it, she is mine.

I love him, she thought, I love him. . . .

"My father," he said quietly, "my father died from the effects of a serious wound that plagued him for three years after the war. I was a year old when he died. And my mother soon followed him. That's all I know about it. I learned about all this one day when I had to be told that the woman I had always thought of as my mother wasn't my mother at all. I grew up with an aunt, a sister of my mother's who had married an attorney. He made good money, but we were always terribly poor. He drank. I took it so much for granted that a man should come to the breakfast table with a thick head and in a foul temper that later on, when I got to know other men, fathers of my friends, it seemed to me they weren't men at all. That there were men who weren't stewed every evening, and who didn't make hysterical scenes every morning at breakfast, was something I couldn't conceive. A 'thing which is not,' as Swift's Houyhnhnms say. I thought we were born to be yelled at, that women were born to be yelled at, to grapple with bailiffs, to fight terrible pitched battles with shopkeepers and go off and open a new account somewhere else. My aunt was a genius. She was a genius at opening new accounts. When things were at their blackest she would become very quiet, take an aspirin, and dash off, and by the time she came back she had money. And I thought she was my mother; and I thought that fat bloated monster with burst blood vessels all over his cheeks was my respected begetter. His eyes had a yellowish tinge, and his breath reeked of beer, he stank like stale yeast. I thought he was my father. We lived in a very grand villa, with a maid and all that, and often my aunt didn't even have small change for a short streetcar ride. And my uncle was a famous attorney. Isn't that boring?" he asked abruptly, getting up to refill the glasses.

"No," she whispered, "no, go on." It took him only two seconds carefully to refill the slender glasses that stood on the coffee table, yet she took in his hands and the pale narrow face and thought, I wonder what he looked like all those years ago, when he was five or six years old or thirteen, sitting at that breakfast table. She had no trouble picturing that fat, drunken fellow grumbling about the jam because all he really wanted was some sausage. When they have a hangover, all they ever want is sausage. And the woman, frail perhaps, and that pale little fellow sitting there, very timid, almost too scared to eat or cough although the heavy cigar smoke caught at his throat; he would have liked to cough and didn't dare because that drunken fat monster would fly into a rage, because that famous attorney would lose control of himself at the sound of that child's cough...

"Your aunt," she said, "what did she look like? Tell me exactly what your aunt looked like!"

"My aunt was very small and frail."

"Was she like your mother?"

"Yes, she was very much like my mother, to judge by the photographs. Later on, when I was older and knew about a lot of things, I used to think: How terrible it must be when he ... when he embraces her, that hulking great fellow with his breath and the burst blood vessels all over his distended cheeks and his nose; she's forced to see them right up close, and those great yellow bleary eyes and everything. That picture haunted me for months, once I had thought of it. And all the time I thought it was my father, and I would torment myself all night long with the question: Why do they marry men like that? And...."

"And you cheated her too, your aunt, didn't you?"

"Yes," he said. He was silent for a moment and looked past her eyes. "That was terrible. You know, when he was seriously ill at one time—liver, kidneys, heart, his insides were all shot, of course —he was in hospital, and we took a taxi there one Sunday morning because he was to have an operation. It was a glorious sunny day, and I was absolutely miserable. And my aunt cried terribly, and she kept whispering to me, begging me to pray for him to get well. She kept whispering this to me, and I had to promise her. And I didn't do it. I was nine, and by that time I knew he wasn't my father, and I didn't pray for him to get well. I just couldn't. I didn't pray for him not to get well. No, I stopped short at that idea. But as to praying for him to get well: no, that I didn't do. I couldn't help thinking all the time how wonderful it would be if . . . yes, I did think that. The house all to ourselves, and no more scenes or anything . . . and yet I had promised my aunt to pray for him. I couldn't do it. The only thing I could think was: Why on earth do they marry men like that?"

"Because they love them," Olina interrupted.

"Yes," he said in surprise, "you know, don't you? She did love him, she had loved him, and she still loved him. At the time, of course, as a young attorney, he had looked different; there was a photo of him taken just after he passed his finals. Wearing one of those godawful student's caps, remember? 1907. He looked different then, but only on the outside."

"How do you mean?"

"Just that—only on the outside. To me his eyes looked exactly the same. Only his stomach wasn't that fat yet. But to me he looked dreadful even as a young man in that photo. I would have seen him the way he was going to look at forty-five, I wouldn't have married him. And she still loved him, although he was a wreck, although he tormented her, wasn't even faithful to her. She loved him absolutely and unconditionally. I can't understand it. . . ."

"You can't understand it?" He looked at her again in surprise. She was sitting up now, had swung her legs down, her face was close to his.

"You can't understand it?" she asked passionately.

"No," he said, astonished.

"Then you don't know what love is. Yes," she looked at him, and suddenly he was afraid of that solemn, wholly altered face. "Yes," she repeated. "Unconditionally! Love is always unconditional, you see. Haven't you," she murmured, "haven't you ever loved a woman?"

He quickly closed his eyes. Again that deep, thrusting stab of pain. That too, he thought, I have to tell her about that too. There must be no secrets between us, and I had been hoping I could keep that, that memory of an unknown face, hoping I could keep that gift to myself and take it with me. His eyes remained closed, and there was silence. He was trembling in his anguish. No, he thought, let me keep it. That's my own most private possession, and for three and a half years it's been all I've had to live on . . . just that tenth of a second on the hill outside Amiens. Why did she have to thrust so deeply and unerringly into me? Why did she have to open up that carefully protected scar with one word, a word that pierces me like a probe, the probe of an unerring surgeon. . . .

So that's it, she thought. He loves someone else. He's trembling, he's spreading his hands and closing his eyes, and I've hurt him. The ones you love are the ones you're bound to hurt the most, that's the law of love. His pain is too great for tears. Some pain is so great that tears are powerless, she thought. Ah, why aren't I that other woman he loves? Why can't I transpose this soul and this body? There's nothing, nothing of myself that I want to keep, I would surrender my whole self to have only . . . only the eyes of that other woman. This last night before his death, the last night for me too because when he's gone I shall have ceased to care about anything . . . ah, if only I could have her eyelashes, give my whole self in exchange for her eyelashes. . . .

"Yes," he said softly. His voice was without emotion, the voice of someone on the brink of death. "Yes, I loved her so much I would have sold my soul to feel her mouth for just one second. I've only just realized this—now that you ask me. And perhaps that's why I was never to know her. I would have committed murder just to see the hem of her dress as she turned a corner. Just something, something real. And I prayed, I prayed for her every day. All lies and all self-deception, because I believed I loved only her soul. Only her soul! And I would have sold all those thousands of prayers for one single kiss from her lips. I've only just realized this." He rose suddenly to his feet, and she was glad his voice was human again, a human voice that suffered and lived. Again the thought came to her that he was alone now, that he was no longer thinking of her, he was alone again.

"Yes," he said into the room, "I believed it was only her soul that I loved. But what is a soul without a body, what is a human soul without a body? I couldn't desire her soul so passionately, with all the insane passion I was capable of, without longing for her just to smile at me at least once, once. God," he slashed the air with his hand, "always the hope, and nothing but the hope, that that soul might become flesh," he cried, "only the insane burden of hope! What's the time?" He turned on her and, although he spoke roughly and brusquely as if she were a servant girl, she was glad to see that at least he had not forgotten her presence. "Forgive me," he added swiftly, grasping her hand, but she had already forgiven him, she had forgiven him before it happened. She glanced at the clock and smiled. "Eleven." And she was filled with a great happiness, only eleven. Not yet midnight, not even midnight, how glorious, how lovely, how wonderful. She was as gay as a carefree child, jumped up and danced across the room: I'm dancing with you into heaven, the seventh heaven of love. . . .

He watched her, thinking: it's strange, really, that I can't be angry with her. Here I am, half-dead with pain, deathly sick, and she's dancing, although she has shared my pain, and I can't be angry, I can't. . . .

"You know what?" she asked, suddenly pausing. "We must have something to eat, that's what we need."

"No," he said, appalled. "No."

"Why not?"

"Because then you'd have to leave me. No, no," he cried out in anguish, "you mustn't leave me for a single second. Without you . . . without you . . . without you I can't go on living!"

"What?" she asked, without knowing which word her lips were forming, for a delirious hope had sprung up within her.

"That's right," he said softly, "you mustn't go away."

No, she thought, that's not it after all. I'm not the one he loves. And aloud she said: "I don't have to go away! There's food too in the closet."

How miraculous, that somewhere in a drawer of that closet

there should be cookies, and cheese wrapped in silver foil. What a glorious meal, cookies and cheese and wine. He didn't like his cigarette. The tobacco was dry, and it had a kind of foul army taste.

"Give me a cigar," he said, and needless to say there was a cigar there too. A whole box of cigars good enough for a major, all for the Lvov mortgage. It felt good to stand there on the soft carpet, watching Olina arrange the little snack on the coffee table with gentle, loving hands. When she had finished, she suddenly turned to him and looked at him with a smile: "You couldn't go on living without me?"

"No," he said, and his heart was so heavy he couldn't laugh, and he thought: I ought to add now: because I love you, and that would be true and it would not be true. If I said it I would have to kiss her, and that would be a lie, everything would be a lie, and yet I could say with a clear conscience: I love you, but I would have to give a long, long explanation, an explanation that I don't know myself yet. Always those eyes of hers, very gentle and loving and happy, the opposite of the eyes I desired ... still desire ... and he repeated, looking straight into her eyes: "I couldn't go on living without you," and now he was smiling. ...

At the very moment when they were raising their glasses to drink a toast to their birthdays or their wasted lives, at that very moment their hands began to tremble violently; they put down their glasses and looked at one another in dismay: there had been a knock at the door. ...

Andreas held back Olina's arm and slowly stood up. He strode to the door, taking only three seconds to reach it. So this is the end, he thought. They're taking her away from me, they don't want her to stay with me till morning. Time is still alive, and the world is turning. Willi and the blond fellow are each in bed with a girl somewhere in this house, that old woman is downstairs lying in wait for her money, the slot of her mouth always open, slightly open. What shall I do when I'm alone? I shan't even be able to pray, to go down on my knees. I can't live without her, because I do love her. They mustn't do that. ...

"Yes," he asked softly.

"Olina," came the madame's voice. "I have to speak to O-lina."

Andreas looked around, pale, aghast. I'll give up the five hours if only I can spend just one more half-hour with her. They can have her then. But I want to spend one more half-hour with her, and look at her, just look at her, maybe she'll play the piano again. Even if it's only, I'm dancing with you into heaven. . . .

Olina smiled at him, and he knew from that smile that she would stay with him whatever happened. And yet he was scared, and he knew now, as Olina quietly unlocked the door, that he did not want to part with this fear for her. That he loved this fear too. "Leave your hand in mine, at least," he whispered as she was going out, and she left her hand in his, and he heard her outside beginning to talk to the madame in hurried, heated Polish. The two women were locked in combat. The moneybox was doing battle with Olina. He anxiously scanned her eyes when she came back without closing the door. He did not let go of her hand. She had turned pale too, and he could see that her confidence was no longer very great. . . .

"The general's turned up. He's offering two thousand. He's furious. He must be raising the roof down there. D'you have any money left? We have to make up the difference, otherwise. . . ."

"Yes," he said; he hastily turned out his pockets, which still contained money he had won from Willi at cards. Olina twittered something in Polish through the door. "Hurry," she whispered. She counted the bills. "Three hundred, right? I haven't a thing! Not a thing!" she said frantically. "Yes I have, here's a ring, that's five hundred. It's not worth more than that. Eight hundred."

"My coat," said Andreas, "here it is."

Olina went to the door with the three hundred, the ring, and the coat. She was even less confident on her return.

"She reckons the coat's worth four, only four—no more. And the ring six, thank God for that, six. Thirteen hundred. Don't you have anything else? Hurry!" she whispered. "If he gets impatient and comes upstairs, we're sunk."

"My paybook," he said.

"Yes, let me have it. A genuine paybook is worth a lot."

"And my watch."

"Yes," she laughed nervously, "the watch. You still have a watch. Is it running?"

"No," he said.

Olina went to the door with the paybook and the watch. More excited Polish whispering. Andreas ran after her. "Here's a sweater," he called through the door, "a hand, a leg. Can't you use a human leg, a wonderful, superb human leg . . . a leg from an almost-innocent? Can't you use that? To make up the difference. Are you still short?" His voice was quite matter-of-fact, not excited, and he kept Olina's hand in his.

"No," came the madame's voice from outside. "But your boots. Your boots would make up the difference."

It's hard work, taking off one's boots. But he managed, just as he had managed to pull them on quickly when the Russians came roaring up to the position. He took off his boots and passed them out by way of Olina's small hand.

And the door was shut again. Olina stood before him, her face quivering. "I have nothing," she wept, "my clothes belong to the old woman. So does my body, and my soul—she doesn't want my soul. Only the Devil wants souls, and humans are worse than the Devil. Forgive me," she wept, "I have nothing."

Andreas drew her towards him and softly stroked her face. "Come," he whispered, "come, I'll make love to you. . . ." But she raised her face and smiled. "No," she whispered, "no, never mind, it's not important."

Again footsteps approached along the corridor, those confident, unswerving footsteps, but strangely enough they were no longer afraid. They exchanged smiles.

"Olina," the voice called outside the door.

More Polish twittering. Olina smiled at him over her shoulder: "When do you have to leave?"

"At four."

She closed the door, without locking it, came back, and said: "At four the general's car is coming to pick me up."

Her trembling hands had spilled wine over the cheese, so she cleared it away, gathered up the soiled tablecloth, and rearranged the things. The cigar had not gone out, thought Andreas, who was watching her. The world had nearly come to an end, but the cigar had not gone out, and her hands were quieter than ever. "Coming?"

Yes, he sat down opposite her, laid aside the cigar, and for a few minutes they looked past one another, in silence and almost blushing, because they were both terribly ashamed at the knowledge that they were praying, that they were both praying, here in this brothel, on this couch. . . .

"It's midnight now," she said as they began eating. It's Sunday now, thought Andreas, Sunday, and he abruptly set down his glass and the cookie he had just begun; a frightful cramp paralyzed his jaws and hands and seemed even to blind his eyes; I don't want to die, he thought and, without realizing it, he stammered, like a weeping child: "I . . . I don't want to die."

I must be mad to think I can smell paint so vividly . . . I was barely seven at the time they painted the garden fence: it was the first day of school holidays, and Uncle Hans was away, it had rained in the night, and now the sun was shining in that moist garden . . . it was so wonderful . . . so beautiful, and as I lay in bed I could distinctly smell the garden and the paint, for the painters had already started painting the fence green . . . and I was allowed to stay in bed a while . . . because school was out, Uncle Hans was away, and I was to get hot chocolate for breakfast, Aunt Marianne had promised me the night before because she had just opened a new account . . . whenever we opened a new account, a brand-new one, we began by buying something special. And that paint, I can smell it as plainly as anything, but I must be mad . . . there can't possibly be a smell of green paint here. That pale face across from me, that's Olina, a Polish prostitute and spy . . . nothing here in this room can smell so cruelly of paint and conjure up that day in my childhood so vividly. "I don't want to die," stammered his mouth. "I don't want to leave all this behind . . . no one can force me to get onto that train going to . . . Stryy, no one on earth. My God, maybe it would be a mercy if I did lose my mind. But don't let me lose it! No, no! Even though it hurts like hell to smell that green paint now, let me rather savor this pain than go mad . . . and Aunt Marianne's voice telling me I can stay in bed a while . . . since Uncle Hans is away. . . ."

"What's that?" he asked, startled. Olina had risen, without his noticing it; she was sitting at the piano, and her lips were quivering in her pale face.

"Rain," she said softly, and it seemed to cost her an unspeakable effort to open her mouth, she hardly had the strength to nod toward the window.

Yes, that soft rushing sound that roused him with the power of a sudden burst of organ music . . . that was rain . . . it was raining in the brothel garden . . . and on the treetops where he had seen the sun for the last time. "No!" he cried as Olina touched the keys, "no," but then he felt the tears, and he knew he had never cried before in his life . . . these tears were life, a raging torrent formed from countless streams . . . all flowing together and welling up into one agonizing outburst . . . the green paint that smelled of holidays . . . and the terrible corpse of Uncle Hans laid out in its coffin in the study, shrouded in the heavy air of candles . . . many, many evenings with Paul and the hours of exquisite torment spent trying to play the piano . . . school and war, war . . . war, and the unknown face he had desired, had . . . and in that blinding wet torrent there floated, like a quivering disk, pale and agonizing, the sole reality: Olina's face.

All this because of a few bars of Schubert, making it possible for me to cry as I have never cried in my life, to cry as maybe I only cried when I was born, when that dazzling light threatened to cut me in two. . . . Suddenly a chord struck his ear, a chord that shook him to the depths of his being, it was Bach, yet she had never been able to play Bach. . . .

It was like a tower that was spiraling upward from within, piling level upon level. The tower grew and pulled him with it, as if it had been hurled up from the bowels of the earth by a gushing spring that was fiercely shooting its way past the gloom of centuries into the light, into the light. An aching happiness filled him as, against his will yet knowingly and consciously, he was borne upward on level after level of that pure, upthrusting tower; as if borne on a cloud of fantasy, wreathed in what seemed a weightless, poignant felicity, he was yet made to experience all the effort and all the pain of the climber; this was spirit, this was clarity, little remained of human aberration; a fantastically clean, clear playing of compelling force. It was Bach, yet she had never been able to play Bach . . . perhaps she wasn't playing at all . . . perhaps it was the angels . . . the angels of clarity, singing in towers each more ethereal and radiant than the last . . . light, light, O God . . . that light. . . .

"Stop!" he cried out, and Olina's hands recoiled from the keys as if his voice had torn them away. . . .

He rubbed his aching forehead, and he saw that the girl sitting there in the soft lamplight was not only startled by his voice: she was exhausted, she was weary, infinitely weary, the towers she had had to climb with her frail hands had been unimaginably high. She was just tired, the corners of her mouth twitched like those of a child that is too tired even to cry; her hair had loosened . . . she was pale, and deep shadows encircled her eyes.

Andreas moved toward her, took her in his arms, and laid her on the sofa; she closed her eyes and sighed; gently, very gently she shook her head as if to say: just let me rest . . . all I want is to rest a little. . . . Peace, and it was good to see her fall asleep; her face sank to one side.

Andreas rested his head in his hands on the little table and was also aware of an infinite weariness. It's Sunday, he thought, one o'clock in the morning, three more hours to go, and I must not sleep, I will not sleep, I shall not sleep; and he looked at her ardently and tenderly. That pure, gentle, small, wan girlish face, now faintly smiling in the bliss of sleep. I must not sleep, thought Andreas, yet he could feel his weariness bearing relentlessly down on him. I must not sleep. God, don't let me fall asleep, let me look at her face. . . . I needed to come to this brothel in Lvov, I needed to come here to find out that there is such a thing as love without desire, the way I love Olina . . . I must not fall asleep, I must look at that mouth . . . that forehead and those exhausted, golden, delicate wisps of hair over her face and the dark shadows of indescribable exhaustion around her eyes. She played Bach, to the very limits of human capacity. I must not fall asleep . . . it's cold . . . the cruel hostility of the morning is already waiting behind the dark curtains of the night. It's cold, and I have nothing to cover her with . . . I've flogged my coat, and we made a mess of the tablecloth . . . it's lying around somewhere stained with wine. My tunic, I could put my tunic over her . . . I could cover the open neck of her dress with my tunic, but even as he thought this he simply felt too tired to get up and take off his tunic . . . I can't even lift my arm, and I must not fall asleep; I've still got so many things to do, so many things to do. Just let me rest here a bit with my arms on the table, then I'll get up and put my tunic over her, and I'll pray, pray, kneel by this couch that has seen so many sins, kneel by that pure face from which I had to learn that there is such a thing as love without desire . . . I must not fall asleep . . . no, no, I must not fall asleep. . . .

His awakening gaze was like a bird that suddenly dies high up in the air in flight and plunges, plunges into the infinity of despair; but Olina's smiling eyes caught him as he fell. He had been desperately afraid that it was too late . . . too late to hurry to the appointed place. Too late to hurry to the only rendezvous that mattered. Her smiling gaze caught him, and she answered the unspoken yet anguished question, saying softly:

"It's three-thirty . . . don't worry!" And only now did he feel her light hand resting on his head.

Her face lay on the same level as his, and he hardly needed to move his head to kiss her. It's a pity, he thought, that I don't desire her, a pity that it's no sacrifice for me not to desire her, no sacrifice not to kiss her and not to long to sink down into that seemingly sullied womb. . . .

And he touched her lips with his, and there was nothing. They exchanged smiles of amazement. There was nothing. It was like an ineffectual bullet bouncing off armor of which they themselves were not aware.

"Come on," she said softly, "I'd better see you get something for your feet, hadn't I?"

"No," said Andreas, "don't leave me, you mustn't leave me for a single second. Never mind the shoes. I can just as well die in my socks, lots of men have died in their socks. Fled in panic when they were suddenly confronted by the Russians, and died wounded in the back, facing Germany, wounded in the back, the worst disgrace that could befall the Spartans. Many died like that, never mind the shoes, I'm so tired. . . ."

"No," she said, glancing at her watch. "I could have given up my watch, and you would have kept your boots. One always thinks one has no more to give, and I honestly had forgotten my watch. I'll trade my watch for your boots, we won't be needing it any more . . . or anything else."

"Or anything else," he repeated under his breath, and he raised his eyes and looked around the room, and for the first time he saw how pitiful it was, the ancient wallpaper and meager furniture: old armchairs over there by the window, and a dingy couch.

"Yes," Olina murmured, "I'm going to get you away. Don't look so scared!" She smiled, her eyes close to his white, tired face. "That car of the general's is a gift from heaven. Just trust me and believe me: no matter where I take you, it will be life. Do you believe me?" Andreas nodded in bewilderment, and she repeated, her face close to his as if in solemn entreaty: "No matter where I take you, it will be life. Trust me!" She clasped his head. "There are tiny little places in the Carpathians where no one will ever find us. A few houses, a little chapel, no partisans even. I used to go to one, I would try to say a few prayers and play on the priest's old baby grand. D'you hear?" She sought his eyes, but his gaze was still roaming the soiled wallpaper against which bottles had been smashed and sticky fingers had been wiped. "We'll have music, d'you hear?"

"Yes," he groaned. "But the others, those other two. I can't leave them now. It's impossible."

"That's out!"

"And the driver," he asked, "what did you intend doing with the driver?" They stood face to face, and there was something like hostility between their eyes. Olina tried to smile. "Starting today," she said softly, "starting today I'm not going to hand over any more innocent men to the executioner. You must trust me! It wouldn't have been too difficult just with you. Simply have the driver stop somewhere, and then we'd run away ... disappear! Free, just disappear! But with your two friends it won't work."

"All right, then you'll have to leave me. No," he raised his arm to silence her. "I'm simply telling you there's to be no bargaining. It's either—or. You must understand, you must," he said, looking deep into her serious eyes, "because you loved them, some of them, didn't you? You must understand."

Slowly, heavily, Olina's head drooped. Andreas did not realize this was a nod until she said: "All right, I'll try...."

While Olina, her hand on the door, waited for him, he cast one more look around that dirty little Polish bar, then followed her out into the ill-lit corridor. But the room, the bar, was palatial compared with that corridor in the early morning. That mocking, chill, dingy half-light in a brothel corridor at four in the morning. Those doors, like doors in a barracks, all alike. All equally shabby. And that dreary, dreary squalor.

"In here," said Olina. She pushed open one of the doors and there was her room: scantily furnished with the necessities of her trade; a bed, a small table and two chairs, and a washbasin on a spindly, three-legged stand, next to the stand a pitcher, and a small closet against the wall. Only the bare necessities, like in a barracks....

It was all so unreal, sitting on the bed and watching Olina wash her hands, take her shoes out of the closet, remove her red slippers, and put on her shoes. Oh yes, there was a mirror too, for her to refurbish her beauty. Those traces of tears must be wiped away and fresh powder put on, there being nothing ghastlier than a red-eyed whore. Lipstick and eyebrow pencil had to be reapplied, nails cleaned, and all this was carried out as deftly as a soldier preparing for the alert.

"You must trust me," she said in a chatty, matter-of-fact tone. "I'm going to get you away, d'you hear? It won't be easy if you insist on taking along the other two, but it can be done. A lot can be done. . . ."

Don't let me go out of my mind, Andreas prayed, don't let me go out of my mind in this brutal attempt to grasp reality. The whole thing is impossible, this room in a brothel, shabby and faded in the gray dawn, full of revolting smells, and that girl over there by the mirror, crooning softly, crooning to me, while her fingers skillfully touch up the red on her lips. This is impossible, and this tired heart of mine that wishes for nothing, and these limp senses of mine that desire nothing, neither to smoke nor eat nor drink, and my soul that is deprived of all longing and wants only to sleep, to sleep. . . .

Maybe I'm already dead. Who can grasp all this, these bedclothes I automatically pushed aside, the way one always does if one has to sit down on a bed, these sheets that are not dirty and yet not clean, these horribly mysterious sheets, not dirty and not clean. . . and that girl over there by the mirror, busy coloring her eyebrows, black, fine-drawn eyebrows on a pale forehead.

"A-hunting and fishing we will go, like in the good old days! D'you know that one?" asked Olina with a smile. "It's a German poem. 'Archibald Douglas.' It's about a man who was exiled from his native land. And we Poles, we have been exiled *into* our native land, into the midst of one's native land; no one knows what that means. Born 1920. A-hunting and fishing we will go, like in the good old days. Listen!" She was actually crooning that old ballad, and it seemed to Andreas that now the limit had been reached, a gray cold morning in a Polish brothel, and a ballad, set to music by Löwe, being crooned for his benefit. . . .

"Olina!" came that level voice again outside the door.

"Yes?"

"The bill. Hand it out to me, please. And get ready to leave, the car's at the door. . . ."

So this is the reality, the girl handing out the bill through the door, with tapering fingers, a bill on which everything had been written down, beginning with the matches, which he still had in his pocket, those matches he had been given yesterday evening at six. That's how fantastically fast time goes, this time we cannot grasp, and I've done nothing, nothing, in that time, and there's nothing I can do but follow this refurbished beauty, down the stairs to settle the account. . . .

"These Polish tarts," said Willi, "simply terrific! That's what I call passion, eh?"

"Yes."

The room downstairs was just as meagerly furnished. A few rickety chairs, a bench, a threadbare carpet that looked like frayed paper, and Willi was smoking. He was completely unshaven and was searching his luggage for more cigarettes.

"You were certainly the most expensive, my lad. My bill wasn't much less either. But this young friend of ours, he cost almost nothing. Hey there!" He dug the blond fellow, who was still asleep, in the ribs. "A hundred and forty-six marks." He snorted with laughter. "It seems he actually did sleep with the girl, literally slept. There were two hundred marks left over, so I slid them under the door of his girl's room, as a tip, see? Because she made him happy so cheaply. D'you happen to have a cigarette left?"

"Yes."

"Thanks."

What an incredibly long time Olina was taking to settle the account, over there in the madame's office, at four in the morning.

That was an hour when the whole world slept. Even in the girls' rooms all was quiet, and downstairs in the big reception room it was quite dark. The door from which the music had come was dark, and one could see and smell that dark room. The only sound was the discreet engine purring away outside. Olina was behind that reddish door, and it was all reality. It had to be reality. . . .

"So you think this general's whore-car will take us too?"

"Yes!"

"Hm. A Maybach, I can tell by the engine. Nifty job. Mind if I go ahead and speak to the driver? He's sure to be a noncom."

Willi shouldered his luggage and opened the door, and there it really was, the night, the gray-veiled night and the dim headlamps of a waiting car out there by the entrance. As coldly and inescapably real as all war-nights, full of cold menace, full of horrible mockery; out there in the dirty holes . . . in the cellars . . . in the many, many towns cowering in fear . . . summoned up, those appalling nights that at four in the morning have achieved their most deadly power, those ghastly, indescribably terrible war-nights. One of these was there outside the door, a night full of terror, a night with no home, not even the smallest, smallest warm corner to hide in . . . those nights that had been summoned up by the resounding voices. . . .

So she really believes she can rescue me. Andreas smiled. She believes it is possible to slip through the fine mesh of this net. This child believes there is such a thing as escape . . . she believes she will find ways to avoid Stryy. That word has been cradled within me since my birth. It has lain deep, deep down, unacknowledged and unawakened; it was with me when I was still a child, and maybe a dark shudder rippled through me, many years ago in school, when we learned about the foothills of the Carpathians and I read the words Galicia and Lvov and Stryy on the map, in the middle of that yellow-white patch. And I've forgotten that shudder. Maybe, often and often, the barb of death and summons was cast into me without ever catching in anything down there, and only that tiny little word had been set up and saved up for it, and finally the barb caught. . . .

Stryy . . . that tiny little word, terrible and bloody, has surfaced and expanded into an ominous cloud that now overshadows everything. And she believes she will find ways of avoiding Stryy. . . .

Besides, her promise doesn't attract me. I'm not attracted by that little village in the Carpathians where she proposes to play on the priest's piano. I'm not attracted by that seeming security . . . all we have is promises and pledges and a dark uncertain horizon over which we have to plunge to find security. . . .

At last the door opened, and Andreas was surprised by the rigid pallor of Olina's face. She had put on a fur coat, a charming little cap was perched on her beautiful loose hair, and there was no watch on her wrist, for he was wearing his boots again. The account had been settled. The old woman was smiling so mysteriously. Her hands were folded across her desiccated body, and after the soldiers had picked up their luggage and Andreas was opening the door she smiled and uttered a single word: "Stryy," she said. Olina did not hear it, she was already outside.

"I too," said Olina in a low voice as they sat side by side in the car, "I too am condemned. I too have betrayed my country because I spent all last night with you instead of sounding out the general." She took his hand and smiled at him: "But don't forget what I told you: no matter where I take you, it will be life. Right?"

"Right," said Andreas. The whole night ran through his memory like a smooth thread being reeled off, yet there was one knot that left him no peace. Stryy, the old woman had said, and how can she know that Stryy . . . he hadn't said anything about it to her, and still less would Olina have mentioned that word. . . .

So this is supposed to be reality: a discreetly purring car with its subdued headlamps lighting up the nameless road. Trees, and now and again houses, all saturated with gray darkness. In front of him those two necks, encircled by sergeants' braid almost identical, solid German necks, and the cigarette smoke drifting back from the driver's seat. Beside him the blond fellow, sleeping like a child worn out by playing, and on the right the steady gentle contact with Olina's fur coat and the smooth thread of the memory of that lovely night sliding by, faster and faster, and always stopping short at that strange knot, at the place where the old woman had said: Stryy....

Andreas leaned forward to look at the softly lit clock on the dashboard, and he saw it was six o'clock, just on six. An icy shock ran through him, and he thought: God, God, what have I done with my time, I've done nothing, I've never done anything, I must pray, pray for them all, and at this very moment Paul is walking up the altar steps at home and beginning to recite: Introibo. And on his own lips too the word began to form: Introibo.

But now an invisible giant hand passed over the softly gliding car, a terrible, silent stirring of the air, and into this silence came Willi's dry voice, asking: "Where are you taking us, bud?" "To Stryy!" said a disembodied voice.

And then the car was slashed by two raging knives that rasped with savage hatred, one from the front, the other from behind, tearing into that metal body which reared and turned, filled with the shriek of fear of its occupants....

In the silence that followed there was no sound but the passionate devouring of the flames.

My God, thought Andreas, are they all dead?... and my legs ...my arms, is only my head left?... is no one there?... I'm lying on this bare road, on my breast lies the weight of the world, so heavily that I can find no words to pray....

Am I crying? he thought suddenly, for he could feel something moist running down his cheeks: no, something was dripping onto his cheeks; and in that ashen morning light, which was still without the yellow mildness of the sun, he saw that Olina's hand was hanging down over his head from a fragment of the car, and that blood was dripping onto his face from her hands, and he was past knowing that now he was really beginning to cry....

EUROPEAN CLASSICS

❧

Honoré de Balzac
The Bureaucrats

Heinrich Böll
And Never Said a Word
End of a Mission
Irish Journal
The Train was on Time

Lydia Chukovskaya
Sofia Petrovna

Aleksandr Druzhinin
Polinka Saks · The Story of Aleksei Dmitrich

Konstantin Fedin
Cities and Years

Marek Hlasko
The Eighth Day of the Week

I. Grekova
The Ship of Widows

Ignacy Krasicki
The Adventures of Mr. Nicholas Wisdom

Karin Michaëlis
The Dangerous Age

Andrey Platonov
The Foundation Pit

Arthur Schnitzler
The Road to the Open